delible

anne stone

serotonin
b o o k s

INSOMNIAC PRESS

Library and Archives Canada Cataloguing in Publication

Stone, Anne, 1969-   Delible / Anne Stone.

ISBN 978-1-897178-36-2

I. Title.
PS8587.T659D44 2007   C813'.54   C2007-901106-3

The publisher gratefully acknowledges the support of the
Canada Council, the Ontario Arts Council and the Department
of Canadian Heritage through the Book Publishing Industry Development Program.

Printed and bound in Canada

Insomniac Press, 192 Spadina Avenue, Suite 403
Toronto, Ontario, Canada, M5T 2C2
www.insomniacpress.com

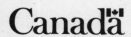

delible

anne stone

Also by the author

Hush
jacks: a gothic gospel

The world is gone
I must carry you

— Paul Celan

Part One

— I —

Melora Sprague

Lying on my back, a handful of dirt in my mouth. Lying on my back, very still, and the dirt inside my mouth is the same as the dirt beneath me. This is my first and most lasting taste of devotion. The sensation against which I measure all other increments of love. My sister kneels beside the body. Her hands move with the delicacy of clockwork. The air is still and cool and the sky is a soft and wintry blue. September. My sister places one twig and then another inside of my open mouth. In two days, she will be nine and then most of a year will have to pass before we are the same, though to Melissa, there is a world of difference between eight and a bit and *nearly* nine.

It's an old game. A game even dogs can play. I am playing dead and my sister fills my mouth with dirt and broken twigs and tiny rocks. Only if I believe I am dead, truly dead, will I not flinch. My mouth is open to each small indignity her fingers offer up.

A few little girls gather around us. Melissa shushes them and demands they lower their heads. One of them, Carly, has a look about her that Melissa likes and she lets that special one sit next to her as she attends to me. Three or four little girls, enthralled by the mystery of a body at rest, form a tiny cabal, gather the heads of dead grass gone to seed. Melissa tells them the dried seeds are my medicine.

I take tiny breaths through my nose. Concentrate on my chest, which must remain still and flat and unmoving until Melissa is ready for me to be saved. Melissa's fingertips trace my eyelids, my cheeks. We are at the centre of another world entirely. A world where seeds of grass, leached out to the colour of sand, restore life. Melissa clears the dirt and twigs from my mouth, and whispering over the shut-eye seeds, places them on my tongue. My eyes are closed, but I can feel her eyes moving over me. Delicious shivers course through my skin. I don't want to be brought back. I want to die here forever.

It's a sniff of gasoline, prickling up through your skin. It's having your hair stroked and your back tickled by the girl behind you as the teacher reads a story and the words run together into the sound of something soft and warm, low to the ground. It's cool cotton sheets fluttering lightly over your body as if Mom has forgotten all about you and set about making an empty bed, only to discover you inside, the sheets so safely tucked, so tight and cool against your skin.

"Snug as a bug in a rug," she says.

My body is the empty bed.

My sister places the last of the seeds on my tongue, and waits for the miraculous rebirth. But I don't come back to her. I *won't* come back. She traces her fingers against my eyelids and, covering my face from view, brutally pinches my nose. And I gasp and choke, undeniably alive.

It's an impressive performance and my sister looks grim but pleased. I turn my back and hork up gravel and dirt, pick the grit from my teeth. The little girls have already forgotten me and turn all of their attention to Melissa, the source of this wondrous gift. They gasp and beg, *me please, me please*. Each wants to lie down in the soft light of Melissa's eyesight and, like Sleeping Beauty, display the still repose of a well-attended corpse.

Mel's eyes scan the playground and she pulls out clumps of grass by the roots. Woodrow Kun-zli stares back at her. His arms reach up over his head, his hands clasp the chain-link fence. He pulls the weight of his body against his arms, stretches, pretends he hasn't been watching her all along.

"Such an odd little boy," Mel says.

I look away from the Woodsman and take her in. It's such a weirdly adult thing for Mel to say.

On my first day of grade three, Woodrow Kunzli is assigned to be my homework buddy. As the odd ones out in the split three-four class, me and the Woodsman are balled together like a couple of orphaned socks in the back of the drawer. I'd tried to catch Mel's eye, but she and Ronnie, also in the fourth grade, are already pushing their desks together. And so, together, the Woodsman and I discover π, measuring the diameter and circumference of the old oil drums abandoned in the swampy woods beside the co-op townhouse project I live in.

At recess, I'd sometimes watch the Woodsman. His hazel-flecked eyes reminded me of vacant lots – the kind people assume are empty. But long after the inhabitants have moved on, there is the debris of lives lived, the stuff no one can find a use for, and marking the border of the lot, a wire fence to collect up the bickering pages of yesterday's news.

It'll be years before I have a phrase to express how the Woodsman gets by. It will be from my father that I learn the most important thing I learn in all of high school, maybe in all my life:

In absence of respect, fear will suffice.

When I first see the Woodsman, I'm small and no one's scared of me. But everyone is afraid of the Woodsman. Everyone except me. Long before I understand it as a choice I've made, I decide to respect him.

For now, with the judicious reasoning of childhood, Woodrow is a nursery rhyme come to life. One day, after recess, we return to find the eyes of our dolls inked out with his pen. In Mrs. Basil's split three-four class, our dolls are blind and the Woodsman sits cross-legged, his face to the corner. *Pens are not allowed.* Mrs. Basil says that, in the shower, she scrubs her skin until it is raw, like her father before her, and compliments me because my body doesn't ever break into a sweat. No matter how hot it gets or how hard I run. She points it out to the whole three-four class. "Look at Lora," she says, "no matter how hot she gets, she never perspires."

"Yeah," snickers Mel, "cause she sweats."

Mrs. Basil ushers us into the girls' bathroom and we wash our dolls' eyes out with liquid soap.

Melissa collects these kindergarten girls like the dolls they are, trussed up in floral designs and bussed in from the western verge of the Saug. Newly brought back from the dead, I kick at the dirt with my Kodiaks and two of the little girls, sisters, cry out and fuss over pink knee socks and black patent leather shoes.

"Let's do something else now," I beg Mel, "look at them, they're dressed for church."

"You didn't complain when they were at your funeral."

The sisters' immaculate shoes dusted off, they press up to Melissa and beg in earnest, drawing *please* out for a full two syllables or shooting out *pleases* so quickly in succession that their tiny mouths sound off like a lit string of ladyfingers.

I squat on a patch of dirt, close my eyes, and try to reach into Melissa with my thoughts. *Choose me, choose me.*

Though we look alike, being sisters and less than a year apart, only Melissa needs glasses. Thick glasses. Coke-bottle glasses. Glasses which, when she takes them off, have the magical effect of making this world a remote and illegible place. With that one deft gesture, Melissa can, if not vanish herself, effectively disappear everyone around her. It is a trick she makes use of whenever she needs the world to become softer, more accommodating. Less insistent. It's as if she expects the world to act in accord with the illusion and just back off.

Mom blames Mel's poor eyesight on her habit of watching television, because she sits six inches from the screen. But it's a habit she's acquired precisely because her eyesight is poor.

Her glasses were found. Alongside her knapsack and boots. At Islington station.

I was fifteen years old, barely, and Melissa was practically sixteen when it happened. But we weren't so far apart as that sounds.

Melissa Ann Sprague and Melora Ann Sprague. Melora and Melissa. Our mom named us so that we would sound alike. Of course, people were always shortening our names. I would've liked it if they shortened me to Mel too, but they always called me Lora and called Melissa Mel, as if they wanted to distinguish us more than we would ourselves. Mel was the first born, and so, was supposed to be named for our grandmother, Penny, but Mom didn't want to name her for so little money. "Why don't we just call her *Chintzy* and be done with it?" she said. And so, my sister was named Melissa. Melissa Ann Sprague.

Though Nanna Stokes calls her Melissa, everyone else, by the time she's a teen, calls her

Mel. Throughout, when she's very sweet or someone wants something of her, they call her *Princess* or *Precious*, and sometimes, though not so very often, they call me that too. But really, by the time she's gone, her name is Mel.

— 2 —

Celia Stokes

There's a difference between dirty and untidy. When I first walked into the place, the girl's room was both. It was a girl's room, then, but now it's a private museum, a curated space. These days, under the seeming mess, the room's immaculate. A little over two years have passed, but I smell the faint odour of bleach. My grand-daughter's socks hang from the rim of the hamper, as they did on the day she disappeared, but something about the arrangement is *too* casual. Like wildflowers bought from a florist: they're grown by the flat, nothing random about it. Melissa's concert shirt is as she left it, looking like it was shed the night before and tossed over the chair's back. Though it was white when the girl left us, the shirt has since gone grey from laundering.

I sit on my granddaughter's bed and Karin

works some small area of the room, as though preparing for a belated return. This last time, she stood at the closet door, a plywood board thinly coated with a simulacrum of wood, and scraped at the words that'd been written there with Liquid Paper, a girl's attempt at sophistication: *Sex Pistols, The Vibrators, Violent Femmes.* Each letter formed in a child's hand, each 'i' dotted with a girlish heart. Karin stood and scraped as the two of us talked. By the time I left, the words were gone, leaving only faint scratches.

By the girl's bed, a heart-shaped frame. In it, an American cliché of a man, his face as wholesome as milk and toast. Handsome, yes, and thoroughly innocuous. Whatever image once looked out over the room had been banished and in its place, Karin left the backing, preferring the anonymous but kind-looking stranger provided by Sears.

Two years have passed and, while a number of things have been removed from the room, Karin has made only one addition, an image of her girl newly pressed into the mirror's frame. A renewed connection to her daughter, a semblance, however slim. If I were a stranger, looking for the first time, I wouldn't see anything out of the ordinary. It appears to be a studio portrait of a young woman, growing older, as children do. It wouldn't be until you looked, really looked, that you'd see it's not a photograph at all, but a document. Not something taken, but *made*.

The first picture I have of Melissa is the first picture of her in this world. In it, she's less than a minute old. A Polaroid snapped in the hospital. The colours made soft, the tint and fade of age. I look at the Polaroid and see how the world belonged to this baby girl, as yet unnamed. *Everything* was hers at that moment. I look at that same picture now and can't help but remember Karin too, still so young herself. None of us could have imagined, the moment the snapshot was taken, that anything in this world could hurt that little girl. Could *bear* to hurt her.

When I look at the newest image, the age enhancement, I see that it too tells a story. In a world apart from us, Melissa turns eighteen. Two years after her disappearance, she is the girl in a colour emulsion who wears a pair of pearl earrings and what must be a private school blazer, its emblem sadly illegible. In a parallel universe, the ersatz world of images, a version of my granddaughter thrives.

In that other world, Mel's braces are gone and her imperfect teeth stand corrected. I can't say that I know this girl, though the features are accurate. While it might only be measured in the smallest of increments, each trivial in isolation, somehow, the sum total of my granddaughter has been replaced. This new Melissa is one who has been chosen for a different path in life. Her image has been adopted out into better circumstances.

Sometimes, Karin pulls out the album of Melissa, the one her brother made in the months after her girl disappeared and together Karin and I look at the old pictures, the real pictures. At times, it's the gap between Melissa's front teeth that holds my eye. Another time, it might be a stain on Melissa's shirt, one Karin must not have noticed, or one that must have occurred between the time Melissa left the house and the moment she'd had her school picture taken. Together, we stare at the imperfect girl, the *real* girl, and I wonder if it isn't these flaws that made Melissa vulnerable to the worst of the world. It's hard to imagine the smallest measure of misery inflicted on Mel's counterpart, this smiling stranger with perfect teeth.

Had they provided us with this version of Melissa when she vanished, there might have been outrage, an outcry, something more. As it was, only one article appeared, a fear piece, the kind of atrocity tale told to frighten parents. In it, Fred Irving wrote about what he called "the girl's troubled history," as if there were signs that reveal who among us is tragedy-prone, as if teenage girls aren't *troubled* by definition. No one would have questioned the later version of my granddaughter. One look, and you'd know that, for her to disappear, something would have to go terribly wrong.

Karin tells me she doesn't remember if Melissa said good night. How does a girl vanish? The door to her room closed. The window screen perfectly placed.

Karin tells me she doesn't remember if Melissa ate her dinner that night, or ate nothing. She doesn't remember the last instant she laid eyes on her, in the kitchen or living room or in the corridor, in passing. And she doesn't know, cannot know, how it was or why Mel was not in her bedroom the next morning, though there had to have been a precise moment in time, like the instant in which the first atom was split, a tiny unremarkable breach to which all the misery can be traced.

I sometimes stay the night in my granddaughter's room, but it's only when I've turned the surrogate's face away from mine that I dream of Melissa in the present tense. And in these dreams, no different from Karin's or Lora's, time turns inward and against itself.

Karin tells me that in her dreams, she returns to the house I lived in when my boy was eighteen. She is pregnant with Melissa, though I am unconcerned. Karin stands in the yard. There is a thorny tree, branches unruly and overlong. Whenever she looks at this tree, she says, she is at peace. No matter that the clouds move quickly, flashing light and dark. No matter, as she stares at its miraculous growth, its frenzied bursts of blooming and shedding, that seasons flicker past. No matter that the snow settling on her shoulders one moment evaporates in a quicksilver of heat in the next. When time slows to a more human pace, my son steps outside. His voice is even and continuous, though his approach jags. He walks towards Karin in a series of stuttering, uneven frames. It's in this way that my son will tell her that Melissa is not coming back.

"It's a bad spot you're in," he will say.

They are the same words, exactly, he uses when leaving Karin.

"I'm in a bad spot," he says.

He closes the door. Through the glass, Karin surmises his face from the few features the light suggests. The line of his cheek. The expanse of his forehead. The ridge of his nose. The rest of my son resides in the shadows.

A teenage girl rides into the yard on a bicycle and stands in the weed bed with her back to Karin. She hears the girl but can't see her face. The girl begins to sob and so does she. It almost feels good, she tells me, the sobs so hard, they wrench her body. Karin stares at the back of the girl's head, the girl faces the horizon, and she finds herself wondering if her eyes are even open.

— 3 —
Lora

For weeks after Mel saw *The Day After*, she had nightmares which she'd describe to me in graphic detail. I could picture the radiation wounds opening in my skin. I started calling her the Prophet of Doom and, on sunny days, I'd eat my cereal alone on the patio, the glass door shut. In our house, the TV was *always* on, and at her worst, recounting dreams inspired by made-for-TV movies, it felt like Mel was always on too.

The morning after one of Mel's nightmares, we were eating our Cheerios and Mom said, "You know, Mel, you're looking at the glass like it's half empty," and Mel looked at Mom like she was completely insane and said, "The end of the world? Half empty? What do you mean, half empty? That glass is completely fucking empty. We're all going to die."

"Not this morning you're not," Mom said, making her point with a butter knife, "not if you watch your lip."

Mel shrugged and said something about mushroom clouds and silver linings, and I shut the glass door and sat in the drizzle, concentrating on my cereal, trying to pin down the last little O with the base of my spoon.

The Saug may look beautiful, but over its trim lawns and anorexic gardens, there hangs a quiet. A decorous quiet that polishes some to a fine matte finish, but for others, like Mel, amounts to a shallow petri dish in which all of the world's anxieties are cultured and grown large. Night after night, tucked under this municipal silence, were her dreams of the A-bomb.

Like most of the girls we knew, Mel struggled with the urge to make *something* happen. To pitch small, sharp rocks against the mannered codes she wanted no part of. To lash out against the unavailing lawns and empty dark around us. For teenagers, the Saug isn't a *place* so much as a *state of mind*. It's boredom incarnate, with an angry edge. Even when you drink and do drugs, the bored anger is there, alongside whatever else you happen to feel. Sometimes Mom sees it in the teenagers who live in our co-op, and calls them *shiftless*, as if three hours behind the counter at the Tim Hortons is the cure.

When Mel was in hospital, I thought I found the answer in her left arm. The IV tube was taped down in an S, the slim plastic needle invisible under her skin. I looked at the blue veins that made a map out of the inside of her arm and thought I could see what was going on inside of her. Would she one day cut the skin, I wondered, just to see? But no, Mel didn't. She didn't *cut*. She found another way out from under those arterial maps.

When the moment was right, I'd meant to ask her, in a way that was serious, in a way she couldn't laugh off, why she'd done it. But she was gone before that time ever came.

Mel told me people can't be beautiful the way they are in books, because even if you get *it* right for a second, you can't help but carry on past the moment where a good story is supposed to end. It was only later I understood what she'd meant, that the length of a life dilutes its meaning, that even if you experience a flawless moment, a perfect distillation of self and world, inevitably, it comes to be adulterated by the clutter of a life lived. Your stomach rumbles with a more pressing need, and before you know it, you're a hundred years old, and that flawless moment is recalled dimly, if at all. Like my sister, I had a fifteen-year-old's vision of beauty and a conviction that nothing stays redeemed.

A week after she was released from the hospital, and a week before she disappeared, my sister experienced her own version of perfection. We emerged from the belly of a parade float to find Jules leaning against his car and grinning. Something in the way he looked at her, she said, let her know, simply know, the past had no need of forgiveness and they'd always be together.

My own flawless moment had already come and gone. Inside the parade float, when Mel and I decided we didn't need anyone. I'd write stories and she'd draw pictures to go with them, and it'd be the two of us, together, against the world, and then Jules came along and ruined everything.

− 4 −

Mel and Mom and me lived in a public housing co-op in the McCauley Green, in one of the fifty pea-pod units that made up our concrete village. Our houses were government subsidized. If you didn't know it before you walked through the neighbourhood, you could tell it from the way old couches, blackened at the folds and felted by the wind and rain, had been dragged into yards and arranged as though they were as natural to lawns as pink flamingos. The Saug, the suburb we lived in, could only have been dreamt up in a distant cubicle by someone who owned a car. After the suburb was half built, that someone developed a social conscience, drew up plans for public housing and discharged his conscience by pneumatic post. Soon after, three or four co-ops were hastily erected between Streetsville and the 403. Our sad cluster was bordered by thousands of new houses, all of them huge by comparison, all of them semi-detacheds with two bathrooms and long rolling lawns out back, all of them with children in colour-coordinated socks. Unlike us, these people didn't go on pogey or pay rent. They *owned*. Unlike us, they had garage sales worth attending.

For as long as I could remember, it'd been the three of us, though Mel and me *do* have a dad, and Mom does – or did – have a husband, whether common-law or for real, she didn't say. Of course, you wouldn't know it except for the pictures that used to be around here. After Mr. D'Sousa's stroke, Mom put the pictures of Dad in a box and claims she can't remember where it got to. Mom has always been cagey on the subject of our father and waves her hand vaguely east as she says that the last she heard, he was working at the Don Jail. It's better this way, she tells us, because the best gifts he ever gave anyone in his life were Mel, me, and the LeBaron, "though not in that order," she'd say. Then she'd grin, so we'd know to taste the sugar in her words.

As for the Don Jail, this was the old days, when no one talked about what a decrepit old shithole it was, and how crowding hundreds of men into tiny cages was about as smart as trying to drown a fire with gasoline. At the time, it was *out of sight, out of mind* and *whatever you do, don't give the bastards cable TV*. Nothing made my Uncle Dave madder than the thought of a bunch of guys lounging around a prison in button-down shirts, watching sports on TV all day long.

So we *do* have a dad, even if he doesn't exist as a proper noun to Mom. He's there, in the gaps in her stories, in a series of blanks in the family album. You can tell the pictures *were* there. The borders around the remaining pictures have dulled with age, and so are now closer to yellow. But every few pages, there is a square, pristine and white, marked off with tipped-in corners, signs that this page once held an image of Dad. In my mind, these gaps in the album are replaced by a series of photographs. In the first, Dad leans against the LeBaron. At seventeen, in jeans and a white T-shirt, he looks impossibly lean and young. If not for his 1950s flat-top, he could be one of the boys behind Industrial Arts, the ones who hold their smokes close to the webbing, so their mouths disappear each time they take a drag. Soon, the separate images of Mom and Dad give way to images of them together, standing in the drive, dressed for a dance, or out back at Grandma's, next to a massive bowl of potato salad. But it's the last one that Mel and me liked best. In the last picture, all of us are together. Dad cradles my sister in his arms and I curl up next to them, ballooning the waist of a bright yellow sundress. As with all Polaroids, this one had begun to fade the last time I saw it. The image of the dress looked dulled, as if it, too, had been laundered many times over the years.

Mel loved that photo best of all. She loved to see us all together. Like a *real* family, she'd say. Mel wanted that *real* family more than anything. I felt differently. All I'd ever had was the second-hand idea of Dad, so when it came to the person out there in the world, I could take him or leave him. The same way he did us.

Mel claims to remember Dad. But in her stories, Dad's eyes are grey, and on the back of his driver's licence, tucked away with the papers for the LeBaron, his eyes are written up as blue. Maybe in memories, sad ones, the colour blue washes out to ash. Or maybe Mel didn't just see things in black and white, she remembered them that way too.

Even before Mel was gone, I knew we'd never be a real family again. Still, it's important to believe in happy endings. In spite of her dreams of mushroom clouds, it was Mel who taught me that.

— 5 —

Probably the place Mel was happiest was at Billy V's. For twenty years, Billy had run an animal shelter in his house on Saug Road, a little below Dundas. Mel had been volunteering with Billy since she was twelve, the summer she'd found a sparrow that had been bitten by a cat, a portion of its pink lung slipping out of a hole in its chest to inflate like a sad and sticky balloon each time it drew a breath. Mom, who'd heard about Billy V's, had driven us there, the bird flopping about in a shoebox on Mel's lap.

Mel held the bird in her hands, and with a tiny hook needle and thread, Billy V darned the hole. When he was done, he set the bird down in its box. With its stitching tied off in little knots, threads dangling from its chest, the sparrow looked like a premature experiment in taxidermy. I was sure it would die. Only it didn't. The bird didn't die and Mel, she found her calling, as she put it, to help animals who'd survived the worst of human nature. Twice a week, for the last four years, she'd gone out to Billy V's, and always, she came home with stories about the damaged creatures people brought there, the victims of traffic or invisible glass or little boys and their matchbook souls.

Billy V was the closest Mel had to a guardian angel. Until I met Billy V, I thought that, soon after you turned eighteen, your heart started to shrivel up like the black pit at the core of a plum, as the sweet meat rotted away. Only Billy V was sixty and he was alive to the world, really truly alive. As the walking dead roamed the aisles, dragging instant-this and add-water-that into skeletal carts, Billy would toss oranges and apples behind him. Mel would pluck these bright-skinned fruits from the air and drop each in the cart, and all the while, Billy V would hum an old Gene Autry tune and do a two-step. Billy V and Mel were a lot alike. Billy sang cowboy ballads and danced like a drunk girl in a spit hole of a town full of boys who'd call a man a fag if his shirt happened to be ironed, and Mel, she always smiled as she said "fuck you."

– 6 –

My fairy godmother had the heart of a librarian. Nanna Stokes. My father's mother. A stranger to me in all the ways that counted. But every Christmas and on my birthday, Nanna Stokes shipped me a hardcover wrapped in butcher's paper. Her books were ancient and held more than words. These were books whose dry pages I softly touched and whose brittle insides I sniffed. These were books printed so long ago, I had to cut the tops of facing pages before I could open them to read. I craved old books the way most teenagers desired cigarettes and alcohol and drugs, though these, too, I wanted.

Mom claimed Nanna's books smelled of grey mould, and threatened to donate the lot of them to the Sally Ann. So I kept them under my bed, arranged in a row, spines facing outwards. *The Secret Garden. Little Women. Oliver Twist.* What Mom didn't get was that an old book holds more than printed matter, it holds a memory of each time it's been read. I could return to these books, catch a glimpse of my younger self, a way of seeing the world I'd since abandoned or refined. Once a year, Mom lined Mel and me up against the kitchen door and cajoled us until we'd straightened our backs and, carefully, in pen, measured our growth on the kitchen door frame. But I grew invisibly, too, inside of my head, and that I could measure in books.

Mom objected to Nanna Stokes because she was 'proper.' When Mom was angry, she'd say of Nanna, "that woman may claim to shit Shinola, but it stinks just the same," and if Mom was in a more philosophical mood, she'd say, "Celia Stokes doesn't look like the type to let anything pass between her legs, but the fact is, she *did* give birth to your father," and she'd shake her head and look at us in wonder. Mom may not have been angry at Dad for leaving our world, but she was sure pissed at Nanna Stokes for bringing him into it. Which is why we saw our Nanna just once a year, Thanksgiving, when Mom picked up a dozen support cheques that Mel was disappointed to find were all signed "Celia Stokes."

Mom called Nanna 'proper,' and my uncle referred to Nanna as *an educated woman*, and what that meant, in the practical terms me and

Mel understood best, was vegetarian, and so, each Thanksgiving we were haunted by the ghosts of turkeys-past as we stared at a plateful of dressing. At Nanna's house, the things that words were pinned to were subtly different. Foods as simple as "cheese" appeared on the table in three syllable servings that smelt like old wet dog and derelict sneakers. At Nanna's table, Mom wasn't herself either. She sat stiff as a corpse and behaved like a stranger. And so those yearly dinners went, with Mom quietly examining her fingernails, Uncle Dave working out some new concoction involving Bombay gin and Nanna finishing the virgin drinks she made for me and Mel with tiny paper umbrellas, and us, begging Uncle Dave to slip a little Bombay-kick in our drinks along with an extra shot of grenadine. And all the while, we'd steal glances at the wall Nanna had papered with images of Dad growing up, and wonder who the man was that had left us behind so long ago.

Mel remembers everything, right back to the cradle. Or so she claims. Once, she told me about the night Dad left us. He kissed her on the forehead and again on top of her head, held his finger to his lips, telling her to stay quiet. She watched him open the bedroom window wide and step out and up into the night. Behind him, he left a series of burning footprints, like the trail of a comet. Mel stood up in her crib, held tight to the bars and watched him go. By then, the closest footprint had diminished to a spectral glow and soon, died away altogether. Mel said that when Mom woke up, she found her standing in her crib still, staring out the open window at a trail that had gone cold. I told Mel she had to have been dreaming, but Mel would only say, "Fine. Go ask Mom what she found me doing the morning after Dad left, see where that gets you." But I knew where that would get me and so this question, like a thousand others, remained unasked.

In absence of Dad, there was always Uncle Dave. Every couple of weeks, Mel and I'd wake to find Uncle Dave's drywall truck parked outside and him crashed on the Naugahyde couch, rolled up in the old knitted throw Mom left out for him. He'd stay for a night, sometimes two. After he woke, Mel and I would take his clothes out to the yard and beat them against the wall, throwing up clouds of plaster dust, and he'd sit around the kitchen in an old housecoat of Mom's, looking to all the world, as he put it, like *a flaming queen*. As we beat his clothes, he'd peer out at the yard from behind the cheap beige curtain that came with the unit, which is what everybody in the co-op called the subsidized houses we lived in, not houses or homes, but units, as in Rental Unit 106, and that we called it a *unit* as opposed to *home* is probably part of the reason nobody had bothered to replace the curtain. When people came and went from the co-op, which wasn't often, they left things worse for wear. Not better. Nobody I knew dug in a cedar bush and the only fresh coat of paint came Friday night, courtesy of Maybelline, and if something broke, you wrote a note and slid it under the office door and did the best you could to fix it because it'd be weeks, if that, before somebody would come by with a screwdriver.

In our house, all jerry-rigging was courtesy of Uncle Dave, who'd yell and cuss out the co-op management the whole time. I've never seen my Uncle Dave really angry, except with Jenny, his common-law wife, though sometimes, he'd get a little pissy with Mom if she brought up her ice skates or the way our unit is haunted which, as Uncle Dave should well know, it is.

Mom claimed the ghost was second-hand, left from the last renters, but Mel believed that it was Mr. D'Sousa, who Mom dated after Dad left, and who had a habit of sorting his change on the kitchen table as he waited for her to come downstairs. He'd been a nervous wreck around Mom, and now, was basically done for, since all those jangled nerves had amounted to a stroke and remaindered him, leaving what is called a 'human vegetable' in his place. When I was a kid that frightened me since I tend to understand most things literally, at least, until Mom took me to see him, laid out on the bed like the kind of poor impression you find in a small town wax museum.

Mom didn't bring anyone home after Mr. D'Sousa. She might have been waiting for him to come out of his coma so she could break it off officially. Or maybe she'd grown tired of the way that all the men in her life ever seemed to do was find new and more terrible ways to leave. The point being, whether or not Mel and me were deprived of a Father Figure, first because Dad stepped into the night and later because Mr. D'Sousa was a Coma Victim, and whether or not we were each now Problem Children as a result, what with all our Strong Male Influences falling by The Wayside, there *was* Uncle Dave, and since I was ten or so, he'd made it a point to come to dinner at least once a week so that *specifically* we had no excuse.

Mom explained it all to us back when I was in grade seven. Mel was laying roads into her mashed potatoes. Mom had made our favorite. Like milk, potatoes came out of a box, powdered. Mom was the coupon queen, and the only person I knew who gloated when she saved a dime on a potato. She told us, graphically, how she was going to use the same dried flakes to explode our mice. Mom's plan was to leave the dry flakes in little tins for the mice and later, when they had a sip of water, the flakes would expand to ten times their normal size.

Kaboom.

No more mice.

Mom waved a forkful of the suspect stuff in Uncle Dave's direction and announced, now that Mel was reaching puberty, the house was in need of a strong male influence, to keep us from "becoming precocious."

"I think she means *promiscuous*," I said to Mel, and Mom gave me *that* look. That fall, Mom had bought me the heavy dictionary I'd been after her for. She hadn't thought words could add up to their weight in sass.

"So, you found one yet?" Mel asked.

"Found one what?" Uncle Dave shifted in his chair to look at her.

"A strong male influence," Mel teased.

"Still looking," Mom said and winked.

Mel was developing a fine wit, and winking was Mom's way of showing encouragement. In my family, if you didn't have a fast wit, you didn't last.

"Precocious," Uncle Dave repeated, rolling up his newspaper. In his mouth, the word sounded frilly and ridiculous, the way Mom's housecoat looked when he wore it.

"Too blinking late," he pronounced, giving Mel a light whack across the head with his copy of the *Sun*.

Mom grinned and Uncle Dave cocked his eyebrow. "What're you smiling at? Where do you think these girls get it from?" He feinted at hitting Mom with the paper, and she laughed and smiled and they both laughed some more. Nobody could be mad at Mom when she smiled. It was like peeling back the rind of an old orange and finding a radiant sun inside. Mom only ever looked tired on the outside.

Uncle Dave was my only uncle. We'd *had* two uncles while Mom was growing up, but before either of us was born, the youngest, Sean, fell through the ice while skating and drowned, which is something no one talks about and which left one uncle for Mel and me.

In the Christmas pictures of Mom as a girl, there's a place on the floor between Uncle Dave and Mom which, if you look at earlier photos, is where Uncle Sean once sat. Mel pointed it out to Mom, the hole in the picture, and Mom looked at it for the longest time. It was as if it was the first time she'd seen the picture. As she put the album away, she said, "He was a good soul, that one, and would have made a good man, better than most," and then she started in on Uncle Dave, who'd pawned her ice skates when he was eleven to buy himself a used guitar that didn't have strings.

"Useless piece of crap," she said, "and when he did get strings, he couldn't play worth a damn, but God, those were a fine pair of skates.

I'd taped tinsel to the heels, and once I was off, that's all I was, a silver blur.

"He used to follow me," she said. "I'd be out on a date and there Dave was, twelve years old and slinking behind, trying to keep up. It was your grandmother who put him up to it, not that he needed much pushing, the little sneak."

"You were with Dad?" Mel wanted to know.

"What do you think?"

"Well, were you with Dad?"

"I could have been a world-class figure skater," she said. "I was *that* good. It was the one thing I *was* good at. The next Petra Burka, that's what everyone said, ask your grandpa, ask your uncle Dave, ask anybody."

"Ask Dad?" Mel asked.

"And completely self-taught. None of these lessons and crap they're pushing on the kids now. Back then, as soon as the first cold snap hit, your grandpa would turn on the hose and fill the yard with water and there you have it, your own personal skating rink. Petra Burka had good ice. I'd like to see her do a triple salchow on the rink in our backyard in a pair of hand-me-down hockey skates. Good luck, lady."

"Then Dave took your skates?" I put in.

"Beside the point. What I did was lose my head to a boy. Lost my sense of balance, too. Of course, the thirty pounds the both of you put on me didn't help. What a pretty picture that would've made, a pregnant ox doing a camel.

"I want better for *my* girls," Mom said, which is what she *always* said after telling a story about having once been young.

– 8 –

As for life outside the family, the day-to-day, most of it had been spent on street corners, waiting for the bus. All that was about to change. Mel was going for her 365 first thing on the Monday she turned sixteen, and that afternoon, she was going to take her driver's test, and on days when Mom could get a ride to work, we were going to drive the old LeBaron to school.

Most mornings Mel and I slept in and missed the school bus, and we had to take the local instead. So to get to first period on time, we needed a car. *Mom's* car. Until then, even if it was an exciting time, as my geography teacher insisted, and the lines on the map were rewritten on a near daily basis, it wasn't like the ground beneath us was going anywhere, Mel said, and besides, we could always catch up later. *With* the car.

Only Mel was wrong.

It wasn't just imaginary borders that were prone to change. A few days before Mel's sixteenth, my sister vanished in a way that felt — even while there were sticky marks from her fingers on doorknobs and crimson traces of her lipstick on glasses in the sink — irretrievable. The ground beneath our feet *had* shifted. Yes, there were givens, facts that did not change. With or without her, I was going to fail geography. Not for the same reasons. Not that I cared.

After she was gone, I'd take the same route to school, but as I got off the bus at Saug Road, I was at the place where the map of Mom's world ends. What with Mel, Mom tore out the part of the bus route map that runs to Islington. So: off limits. If I was lucky, the next bus would be pulling up and if it was stalled at a red light, I'd race across and catch it. As I changed buses, I was off the map. Mom's world disappeared the moment I stepped up onto the south-east corner where the rip begins.

I'd step off the map and my sister's blank smile would be there to greet me. Oblivious to where she is, Mel smiles as daily the poster is eaten into by the wind and rain.

— 9 —

The morning Mel disappeared was one of the few days she *didn't* sleep in. She was gone before I woke. I assumed she'd taken the school bus or slipped out to meet some boy who'd promised to drive her around before school. It wasn't until Billy V called up, after I'd been home from school an hour, that I knew something was wrong. And already, she'd been gone since morning. If not in the night. Mel *never* missed Billy V's.

At 3 a.m., Uncle Dave drove us to the police station to report my sister missing. Officer Groves made it pretty clear that he thought my sister had run away. *Again*. He said he had it on file that we'd been in twice before to report her missing.

He'd put in a report, he said. But beyond that, the best thing we could do was wait forty-eight hours.

"Twice before," he said and shrugged, "and

what with the trip to hospital, I think we need to consider the possibility she'll come home on her own, when she's run out of steam." Mom leaned forward, staring. Her hands holding her stomach. She'd told him about Mel's trip to the hospital to get sympathy, but the officer saw it as further evidence of Mel's unhappiness at home.

Mom pushed back her chair and put a few feet between her and the officer. Uncle Dave followed and laid his hand on her shoulder. "Let's get you a coffee," he said, looking stunned.

"You go ahead," she told him. She looked at me and raised an eyebrow. I walked over to Mom and she said, "That man wouldn't say shit if he had a mouth full of it."

I nodded. Mom could tell that kind of thing about a person, just by looking.

Mom chewed on her lip. I could tell she was thinking things through. "You being here," Mom said, her voice lowered, "it makes him feel bad, you know that."

"Sorry," I said, glancing at Officer Groves.

"No, honey, that's *good*. Your sister needs you. You just keep talking, okay, sweetheart?"

I nodded and Mom turned away, paused, and turned back again. "You remember what we talked about in the truck?"

"Don't worry, Mom. I'll watch my mouth."

She nodded and walked over to Uncle Dave.

A moment later, I was sitting back down across the desk from Officer Groves. "You want to draw or something?" he asked, offering me a pencil.

"Nah," I said, but for some reason, I took the pencil. Officer Groves looked like he was working up to say something, but whatever it was, he let it go.

"You know how Mel's run away before?" Groves nodded.

"That means she's sort of experienced, right?"

He nodded again.

"So she would've known better, I mean, than to run on Thursday when if she waited until Monday, she'd have a driver's licence and birth-day money too, right?" The logic, I thought, was unassailable.

Officer Groves frowned and looked across the room.

"Besides, every other time, she always told me where she was going. She wasn't going any-where this time. We had plans. There's a birth-day party for her Saturday and I don't think she was going to run. Everything's changed. She *was* in hospital, but after that, she's been pretty, uh, *well-adjusted*. I mean, for Mel, she's been really *well-adjusted*."

It was the word Mrs. Buchanan, the social worker, had used in hospital. What she'd wanted for Mel. I planted a row of teeth marks in the soft cylinder of wood. It was soothing to bite down, and I didn't want to cry. Not here. The sterile lights whitewashed our faces and everywhere, I could hear the caterwauling of drunks and while walking me to the bathroom, the officer pulled me out of reach of a man who grinned in an ugly way. Over the last year, I'd learned to hate this place.

The officer shook his head. He must've considered it his bad luck in getting stuck talking to the kid. Groves glanced across the station once more, and this time, I followed his eyes.

Mom and Uncle Dave were standing next to a coffee machine. Every few seconds, she punctuated her point by slamming her open hand against the machine. Uncle Dave looked as if he was trying to maintain a difficult balance or walk a thin yellow line. When things went to shit, Uncle Dave didn't cry. His joints stiffened and his breathing became heavy, audible. Mom, when she got upset, swore and smacked the car's hood or whatever else was close to hand. From where I was sitting, across from Officer Groves, I had a clear view of Uncle Dave, who was trying to convince Mom that it was a bad idea to take out her frustration on the police station's only coffee machine. Soon, Uncle Dave was cursing too, and Mom, she stopped, leaned up against the wall and coolly crossed her arms, as if considering whether or not she'd have to resort to a brown paper bag to get Uncle Dave to come to his senses.

The station house was wide open. Small banisters marked off divisions. Everyone had a clear view of the two of them and it looked to me like they were tagging each other to lose it.

Finally, my uncle calmed down before my mom had a chance to reheat, and Uncle Dave, he folded Mom up in his arms. One of his hands patted the top of her head. I looked up at Officer Groves, but the moment I'd let my focus drift, he'd buried himself in the requisite paperwork. I waited, but pretty soon, I got the feeling he was done with me.

"Here's your pencil," I said and dropped the stub in his mug.

Only Officer Groves either didn't or pretended not to hear.

"She didn't run away. This time *is* different," I repeated, slowly. And in that moment, I understood Mel's second best friend, Val Swynerchuk. What was at the cold dark heart of Val wasn't so cold or dark. I'd found the same dead centre in me. I sat down in the chair and looked at Officer Groves. He was going to hear my sister's story, all of it, and this, I believed, would change everything.

— 10 —

Karin Sprague

Mel was my first.

I was young. Fifteen.

I remember, a girl myself, I'd think about the baby inside of me. Wonder. Picture the tiny hairs on her knuckles and arms and head. Shedding. Didn't know anything about anything. Let alone being pregnant. Couldn't talk to my folks. I was sick. All the time. Uncomfortable. All the time. They say pregnant women glow.

Not me.

The glow came after. When Mel was out in the world with me. She was sweet, my girl. I loved her. More than anything in this world. It came on suddenly, that love. Like a switch flicked on.

That's *my* girl, I said. So small in my hands, I could hold her like this. When I first held my girl, I was a different person. Looked beyond myself. For the first time.

Maybe the last.

Lora came hard on Mel's heels. Like all stupid kids, I made stupid mistakes. I didn't think the plumbing was back in working order yet.

I was too tired to think.

When I found out I was pregnant again, I half expected, as soon as Lora got herself born, I'd feel that same sudden love. The way I had with Mel.

It didn't happen.

I saw myself in Lora. When I looked at her, small as she was, I saw my own eyes staring back. That same expression. It was as if the essence of me had been pushed out into the world, one more time, for a second go. To try and get it right. I'd look at Lora and feel tired. Bone tired.

I'd pinned my hopes to their father. Laid my dreams at his feet. Only the young can give themselves up so completely. He left me at sixteen years old. One girl on the hip and a second on the way. He was gone months before Lora crowned. I didn't have it in me to feel sad. Just tired. Worn out. Empty. They have a label for it now: postpartum depression. At the time, they had a different label: Bad Mother.

The first girl *fought* to get herself born. The second slid out of me with no effort.

In the end, Lora didn't give me half so much

grief as Mel. Lora is the kind to manage. On her own. She has less need of people than most girls that age. Some are born that way, I guess. Needing less from the people around them.

— II —

Lora

Most days we managed to crawl out of bed on time, and Mel and I caught the yellow school bus. The bus takes a road that passes by the last of the farmers' fields, which all the kids say are haunted. Every year, there are signs for a new development posted by the remains of another farm, so it's easy to see farmers as the ghosts they are becoming.

At school, the two of us would go up to the bathroom on the second floor, where rocker girls pass the time before class. We'd squat there, mornings, play euchre and smoke. Each time the door swished open, the smell of smoke and patchouli oil drifted into the hall. Once in a while, Ronnie held her Zippo under the spout of an aerosol can, so a beautiful stream of flame erupted in our midst. And once in a while, though not so often, I'd arrive to find that someone had busted into the tampon dispenser. At times like these, Streetsville truly was the *Land of Bread and Honey*, like the sign next to Vic Johnston's arena says.

It used to be, every day, Val would walk in and say, "Hey, can I bum a smoke." Period. No question mark. And one was produced.

Mel wouldn't give her one. It was always one of the niners who'd cough up.

Mel would look at Val and shake her head and say, "Man, you're such a hyme." But she respected Val's ability to get by on squat, too.

A few months before Mel disappeared, I made the mistake of saying that word in front of Mom. I was looking for my favourite jeans and Mom said Mel had them on when she left for school. I shook my head and said, "Oh man, she's such a little hyme."

"Where do you get this hyme business?"

I chewed my hair and tried to recall the table of chemical elements. We were being tested in second period, and I'd meant to brush up.

Mom didn't wait for me to answer.

"I know where you get it. I know exactly where you get it. You may think that Val girl is something, but she's not. Do you know where she's going? Do you? No place, fast. Those girls are ignorant, ignorant," she said and then she looked into my eyes. What she saw didn't impress her. "You think I don't know? Oh, I know, I know all about those girls. I hear things. I see things. What? You think I'm blind *and* stupid?"

"No, Mom, just blind," I muttered.

Mom halved the distance between us. She raised an eyebrow, gave me *that* look and crossed her arms, waiting me out. I tried to blank out my expression, but when she looked into my eyes, which were the same shade as her own, it confirmed something she knew. It was no use shutting them. I'd tried it, but when Mom was ragging, eyelids were no use. I tried to derail the silence, softly. I had *the* perfect argument in my head.

"But Mom," I began.

"But Mom, nothing. You think the sun rises and sets on those girls' back ends? Let me tell you about those girls. I've seen where they park those back ends of theirs, let me tell you. You think their mothers love them? Letting them dress like that, out at all hours? God knows where, God knows what. I bet you think their mothers do them a real favour. Take Ronnie. I love that girl like she was my own, but honestly, do you think Cathy has done that girl a favour?"

When Mom was pissed off, she was basically psychic. Ronnie's mom *did* do her favours. Working until midnight on weeknights, pulling shifts for most of the weekend, and Mr. Baxter was *always* going out. As far as home went, I couldn't imagine a better arrangement, except say, that *and* a barn. I loved my mom, but she did get in the way of things.

"Look, Mom," I began.

"Don't you take that tone with me, Missy. And don't be expecting any favours," she said. "You think I don't know? I know. I've been to Terry's. I've seen those girls and I've heard those girls talk. Little Miss Know-It-Alls, parking it like they own the place. It's a real shame, I tell you, but lately, Ronnie's no better than the rest."

Every couple of weeks, Mom made us meet her for lunch. The Streetsville Inn, with its juke-box and honeybuns and bottomless pots of tea was our hangout. They never threw us out and the place was stylish in a Stompin' Tom sort of way. Like the waitress, the Inn wasn't beautiful anymore, but you could tell that the place had been pretty once, and still had a lot of character. The walls were covered in a paisley of black velveteen and the waitress had the attitude of a lifer. The cook, a morbidly obese woman by the name of Sarah Lee, had left Streetsville Secondary the year before with the nickname 'Chicken Tits.' Under the black crud that thickened the water faucets, the place had charm, but it was a charm that would have been indecipherable to Mom. So, when we had *Lunch With Mom* we ate uptown, at Terry's.

"Look, all I want is my pants," I got in.

"Forget the pants." Mom shook her head. "What I want you to ask yourself is if you want to spend your time with a bunch of ignoramuses."

I tried, and failed, to look sorry.

"Lora," she intoned, her voice rising in warning.

"Tell Mel," I mumbled, "she stretches everything. You should be telling her."

"Melora Ann," she said, "I know you understand me perfectly."

Mom looked me right in the eyes and it was like she could see inside of my head.

"What I want you to think about is your future," she said. "Where do you think girls like that will end up? Where do you think they'll be when you need to pay rent and make your own way? No place, that's where they'll be."

Mom sighed and sat on the arm of the couch, patting the cushion next to her.

"You know," Mom told me, "the truth is, I worry about Mel because I've always worried about Mel, I've always *had* to worry about Mel, but I never thought you'd be one to worry me. I always thought you had a pretty good head on your shoulders."

It got me when she said that.

"Okay, Mom," I said, sitting down, "sincerely

and truly, I *promise* to be good."

"Do you know *why* what you said was wrong?"

"Yeah, Mom," I said, wanting her to stop. I was dead tired and could care less, and I was no closer to knowing the elements. I tried to picture the periodic table. It was next to a poster of Mussolini above the blackboard. During class, I would say his name over and over, like a poem. When I looked up Mussolini in an encyclopedia, I felt bad. I hadn't meant to have a crush on a fascist dictator. I'd thought he was poet because he was so beautiful you wanted to lick his face.

Mom shook her head and said softly, "Ah geez, Lora, what are you doing? You're my beautiful girl, you know that. Now go and wash that crap off your face. And call that Woodrow boy back." She held up three fingers. "He called three times last night."

"Yeah, Mom."

"Jesus H," she muttered, "you'd think she'd been raised by raccoons."

Mel kept makeup in her purse, so I could put it back on at school. Sometimes, Mel wore her makeup to bed and so did I, and I'd picture our townhouse on fire, the two of us tragic with our eyeliner smudged in the black and white photo the newspaper snapped as we stood on the street in our PJs. While I only had the basics, Mel had it all – a blue stick to colour the tiny line inside of the lower lashes and black for all around. She had lipliners and lipsticks and gloss. She even had a bottle of foundation and a compact. I didn't mind taking the shit off for Mom. Even before Mel was gone, it was important to me to make Mom happy sometimes.

It just never seemed to stick.

I have a theory. I don't know if it goes for everyone, but I suspect that it went for Mel at the very last, and almost always, it went for me.

Among the places you enter, there are the rare ones which change you, because when you stumble in, like Alice into a rabbit hole, all of your personal beliefs are suspended, and new, unfamiliar elements come into play. Say you enter a place that doesn't know your history, without something to tie you down to who you were before, it's pretty easy to become what the room's about. Say one of those rabbit holes winds you up in prison, even if it's through no fault of your own, it won't be long before you start to think of yourself as a prisoner. You take on the characteristics of the place you're in.

If I were going to find Mel, that's how I'd begin. I'd go to the very last place she'd been and become what the place suggested I become. Only Islington station was no help. Islington station was a means to get to Toronto, where you could go anywhere and be anyone. If I wanted to find Mel, I needed to see the station the way Mel had, as the means to an end. If, say, I found out all the places Mel had been before Islington, and went to each, something of where she was headed might become clear to me. That's if Mel had been the one to leave her stuff behind at the subway station. That's if her stuff hadn't been put there to throw us off. Unlike everyone else, I wasn't so sure.

Even before Mel was gone, I'd begun to think about rooms that change you.

When I'd talked about the theory with Mel, she'd said in a withering voice, "You are *so* psychological." I could tell, by the way she said it, that that was a bad thing.

Besides, I'm not psychological.

This was all back when I was in ninth grade and straight ahead as a kid, writing stories all the time. My latest was an end-of-the-world story. In it, a lot of nuclear bombs go off, destroying the planet and leaving everything in ruins. Everything except for 72 Joymar Drive, the address of Streetsville Secondary, a depressing address and depressing thought, but realistic, too, since our high school is basically made out of asbestos and spit. All but one of the characters in my story are aliens, nomads from a distant civilization who land on the ruined earth and decide to live here as the earthlings once had. They adapt to their surroundings, our high school, and fit themselves in.

For the first two days, the aliens are content to leaf through yearbooks and drink Tang, but when they find the war's only survivor, the last living girl on earth, they really get into the spirit of the place. Soon, there's strife and oppression, black and orange gym shorts, and *Health and Guidance* as a required credit.

As much as Mel liked the story, she had her own ideas about the ending. She said to me, "In my version, the story would first of all have pictures, and second of all, I'd base the girl on Ronnie, Val and me, all rolled up into one, and third, the girl would *not* die on day nine. In my version, the girl doesn't die. The girl kicks ass," Mel said, "and through it all, she looks fucking great."

"So, if I made the character a guy, it'd be okay if he dies?"

Mel paused and lit a smoke. "I'm tired of dead girls," she told me. "Girls always die – *always* – especially in your stories. It's depressing. It's like a newspaper, it's so fucking real. I thought people wrote stories so there could be happy endings, not like real life. I mean, why bother?"

"Well," I said, quoting my English teacher,

"art *is* like life sometimes. Sometimes it's even realer than life."

"For such a little runt, you're pretty fucking smug," she said and I flinched.

"You did hate it."

"I'm not talking about your story, I'm talking about *you*. What *you* said is smug, like *I* don't know art. Like *I'm* some kind of art-retard. Maybe I don't get straight A's like some people in this house, but I know art. I draw it all the time," she said, "I make the shit."

I didn't mean to cry, it was pure hormones, but Mel saw my eyes welling, and she took a deep breath. "Look, I don't hate your story," she said. "It inspired me, okay? I liked it. A lot. You even have a point," she said, "you know, with the whole prison *mentality* thing."

"It's the only thing I do," I said, "I make up stupid stories, okay?"

"They're not stupid," she said, and touched my arm. "Look, I'll draw the pictures."

I looked up. Mel smiled and I felt better. Instantly.

"All I'm saying is, you'll have to change the ending because in my version, the girl wears shitkickers. Period."

I looked at her blankly.

Mel shook her head and said, "In the *Coles Notes* version of real life, so you know, shitkickers are Kodiaks."

— 12 —

Seeing Mel with Jules I refined my theory: rooms that make you a stranger to yourself exist *away* from the folks who love you, like Mom and the Woodsman, like Uncle Dave, and these rooms feel more real to you than the person you were before you opened the door and walked inside.

I didn't know we were headed for one of these rooms the night that Jules's Volvo pulled up in front of our unit or I probably wouldn't have gotten in, because that car drove us to a little house on the edge of town, a house of chameleon rooms, and in that house, everything changed. Mel became what it meant for her to be with Jules, and I became what it meant for Mel to be with him, too. Jules, he was getting a tattoo and so, Melissa didn't ask *if* she should get one too, but turned to Jules and asked *what* she should get and with an arsonist's smile, *where*, and when we left the house, those tattoos didn't fade. No, the tattoos were vivid, even as blood seeped through the gauze and pooled under the saran wrap we'd taped over them, and as, slowly, the blood clotted and the surface scabbed up. Months later, after Mel was gone, Claire told me about the Exchange Principle, and it already made sense. Because sometimes, something of the room will stay with you, even as traces of you are left behind. Those traces can be small, like a hair snagged on a hair-brush, but at other times, it's a piece of you that's gone.

When we walked in, the old woman who lived there wanted nothing to do with me. She stopped me in the hall to say she didn't want me dragging her into any of it. She told me to go home, only Mel said *we* were staying. Fine, the old woman told Mel, but if the little one stays, she'd better not go and cry to her mother. Mel shrugged her off and the old woman fingered a cold sore on her lip. On her hand, there was an inky web of lines. The tattoo was uneven, as if she'd shrunk inside of her skin, and she had bruise-dark circles under her eyes.

The old woman sat at the kitchen table, and for the rest of the night, if she so much as turned her head my way, I tried to catch her eye, smile, show her everything was going well, that I was mature for my height, but she'd just shake her head like she wanted nothing to do with me. The old man and his needle warmed to me, but the old woman didn't. Something about Mel and me got on her last nerve, and if anything, her mood grew worse as the night wore on.

"I was young once, you know," she told Mel, shaking her head like there was a bad smell in the room. But it was probably just the cat piss, and besides, it was hard to imagine her ever being young.

Mel had tucked the bottle of Southern Comfort between her legs and she and Jules were kissing hard and sloppy. They didn't seem to remember I was in the room. Soon, they disappeared into Jules's bedroom, bottle in hand, so I retreated to the kitchen, where the old woman leaned into her elbows, an issue of *Cosmo* spread open before her. Darryl stood by the stove, the blackened blade of a knife laid against a hot element, a thin line of smoke rising up.

He offered the next knife to me.

Mel had done hot knives for the first time in the back of Pete Duncan's car. Mr. Correia, our school janitor, must've seen the glow of the blowtorch because he knocked on the window of the car and asked, "Everything all right in there, Miss? You okay in there?"

Pete shook his head, climbed up front, and screeched out of the lot and Mel, jogged by the speed bumps, got sick all over the back window.

A sad miscalculation. She'd thought it was open. I was pretty sure it was the beer and whiskey she'd had that night, and not the knives, but to be safe, I said to Darryl, "Mmm, I dunno."

Darryl looked at me.

"It's just that, I don't know, this one time that Mel did hash oil and she threw up."

"Not hash," Darryl said, "*Kashmir.*"

I looked at the dark vial and Darryl turned back to the stove, knife in hand.

Before Darryl had dropped out last year, I'd see him mornings in the parking lot. Like the Woodsman, he hung out behind Industrial Arts. He'd lean against the trunk of his 1972 Mustang, hand-painted a sunless matte, and dispense drugs and philosophy.

"You know," Darryl was saying, "you're not going to go reefer-madness if you smoke a little. Drugs are like friends. You treat them right and they treat you right."

"So," I said, picking up the vial, "this is like your friend, huh?"

"Yes," he said, and his eyes were serious. "Drugs *are* friends. Unlike people. People want to *change* you. But not drugs, drugs *like* you. And Kashmir, Kashmir doesn't just like you, it has *love* for you. It doesn't try to change who you are. All it wants is your happiness."

"That's very selfless," I said.

Darryl narrowed his eyes and took me in.

"I mean, like, if you think about it, drugs are downright Christian," I added.

Darryl smiled, nodded, like I finally got it.

"Okay, I'll have a little," I told him, since cashmere liked me, or I liked it. The sweaters I liked, and the slow sound of the word, and Darryl too, but to be safe, I said, "Only a little, okay?"

"I don't know where people get this soup-line mentality," Darryl said, shaking his head, "but it's a problem. Look, maybe it's my nature to be generous, and I'm liking the universe right now, and that puts me in the mood to be charitable – fuck it, talking about why people do things is bullshit, motivations are the inventions of lawyers. But to a *thinking* man, motivations are a mystery saran-wrapped in an enigma and Fed-exed to a freaking conundrum. Lies, all of them, bullshit and lies, the shit you come up with after you've fucked up, but the point is, you don't ask to be given shit like it's free, and you don't ask to be given shit like you're doing somebody a favour by taking it, and no matter what anybody says, nothing in this life is free. Not in *this* world."

A smile crept onto the old woman's face.

"It's the oldest scam in the world," Darryl said, "people acting like they give you shit for free. Don't buy it. They're buying you."

Darryl held out the knife and I took it,

grateful he'd stopped talking to me like a stupid kid. As Darryl coaxed the thick substance onto the butter knife, I folded and rolled a newspaper sheet into a cone. I held the knife to the element and Darryl adjusted my hand. When the smoke trailed up, I leaned over, careful not to bring my face too close. Over my shoulder, Darryl whispered, "nice," and "good." I felt him press in close behind me, and pictured the slim options in my panty drawer, which looked like a Biway bin of cheap seconds.

"Get a load of her," the old woman said and I stepped away from the stove, lungs full of smoke, "she thinks it makes her real sophisticated."

I glanced at the old woman, cheeks burning. By way of apology, I offered up a tiny puff of smoke each time my lungs spasmed. The smoke leaked from me, my cheeks deflated like used balloons, and Darryl and the woman, they began to joke like old and good friends, and I got out of the kitchen.

In the living room, Mel and Jules were back at it, tongues moving in tandem, endlessly spinning round. My throat felt rough and my breath kept catching.

Perched on the edge of the couch beside Mel, I unrolled the newspaper and a story caught my eye. I've since wondered if what I read that night was a jinx. The newspaper had a feature about the little Keenan girl, the one who'd been killed that last winter. Only the article was old, because in it, the little girl was alive, or missing still, not yet discovered dead in a rooming house fridge. All our lives, little girls like this one had been disappearing, only to have their names and grade school pictures appear on television screens, in newspapers, and this last year, on the cartons of milk whole families opened each morning and poured over their cereal. This story was old, and like a senile grandparent, asked after a child that had long since been buried in the ground, at least, what was left of her had been.

There was a sad hope in the story, sad, naïve, and mistaken, and for some reason, I started to read it out loud. In the piece, the little girl's father was looking for his daughter, talking right through the paper to whoever had taken his girl. You could tell, right away, how much he loved her.

Mel pulled away from Jules. She looked sad and slightly to blame, the way she did when something she loved, a favourite old mug, unexpectedly broke, cutting her in the process. Jules wiped his mouth on the back of his hand, placed his hand on my arm, and looked at my face. When I looked up, I could see Darryl behind him, standing in the doorway.

"You okay?" Jules asked.

I nodded and wiped the tears from my face, feeling nauseous.

I looked into the eyes of a little dead girl, as she posed for a strip of photo-booth pictures, ones her dad would later give the newspaper reporter, and I suddenly, sharply, missed the father I'd never had. Though she was only a little kid, and making believe, you could see how pretty she was, how she'd be a real looker when she grew up, if she'd grown up, I mean, if she wasn't dead now, too.

− 14 −

I paused in front of the plywood door to read the page that had been pinned there. "Magic Man," written in indelible ink.

"It's the next one over," Darryl said, pointing at Jules's door with his chin. "Go on, I'll be there in a sec," he said.

I looked a second longer at the poster and was startled when the door, open a crack, shut from within. I quickly moved on to Jules's bedroom. Inside, the faint smell of old laundry. Not clean, but denatured by time. A single mattress half-covered by an old stained sheet and beside the bed, a night table that had grown old without becoming more precious. Old and beat-up and without a history that anyone would care about. Sitting on the mattress, I wondered how Mel had felt about doing it on a bed that was no more than a dirty old mattress on the floor, marked by some other girl's period stains, with a guy who owned two books, *Dracula* and *Desires of the Flesh*, where there was a poster of a dirt bike on the wall, and on the bike, a woman with crisped blonde hair sported breasts that looked like they'd been moulded out of wax.

The Polaroids had been slipped into one of the paperbacks. I didn't mean to look at each in turn, but that's what I did. The pictures told a backwards story which ended with Mel smiling, dressed again, her big drunken eyes looking into the camera. She looked pretty and trusting and sweet in the first one. I slipped the photos into my purse. In those days, I was still cleaning up after Mel.

Holding Jules's camera at arm's length, I took a picture. With a tiny whir, the camera spit out a blank portrait. In place of an image, a pearly bronze filled the white frame. As I watched, a girl's features began to emerge, faintly, from the murky plane. The picture, half-made, caught the mood of the place. As the image slowly surfaced in the milky emulsion, so did something of the article on the little Keenan girl, this shithole of a bedroom, and the old lady leaning into an old issue of *Cosmo*. This mood disappeared as the illusion of wholeness took over, and crisp surface features emerged on a static plane. Darryl opened the door, and stood there for a minute, looking at me, sprawled on the bed.

"Scootch," he said, handing me a Blue.

Darryl lay on his back and looked at the ceiling and listened to the story I told him, about two sisters who warm copper pennies in their mouths, and press the warmed pennies to a frosted window, to open up a small view of the world. When I was done he kissed me and slid his hand under my shirt, and unbuttoned my jeans so the T as in Tuesday peeked through the zipper, and I said, "Maybe we should go back now," which he understood as me saying I need another beer first. Which, as it turns out, I did.

When we came out, Jules was holding the bottle in one hand and giving Darryl the victory salute. He made the two-finger gesture over Mel's shoulder as she kissed his neck and I rolled my eyes but Mel didn't notice. Drunk, Mel had all the presence of an afterthought, like it had occurred to Jules, when he was halfway out the door, that a drunk girl, arms wrapped around his neck, might set his boots off nicely.

I squatted by the fireplace. It was stuffed with old two-four cases, pizza boxes and soiled napkins. I knew right from wrong. I knew, for instance, that it was wrong to steal, but I knew that tidying up did not constitute theft. So, as Jules and Mel kissed, and while Darryl rummaged in the fridge for a couple of bottles of teenage foreplay, I tidied all but one of the Polaroids of Mel, tucking them neatly inside of the old pizza box.

Darryl handed me another Blue, squatted and asked, "You wanna see it go up?"

I nodded.

Flicking his silver Zippo, he set blue flames licking at the edge of an old newspaper. The fire slowly crept up and over the pizza box. As smoke poured into the room, Darryl swore and fished for the damper with an iron poker.

Darryl had set the pictures on fire, and it felt right. He'd done the right thing. In the end, I'm not sure why we did what we did next. I don't know if looking at Mel's pictures had demystified if not the act itself, the part that came before it, or if Darryl burning the pictures made me feel closer to him. Maybe he'd been right all along, and all I'd needed was a few beers. The math's the same in any case, so I guess why a person does what they do doesn't matter.

The tattoos came after.

The tattoos came after Jules had made the victory sign for a second and final time, and it was only later, much later, that I realized Mel's tattoo could mean one thing for her, after she'd left, but all along, might mean another thing entirely to Jules.

— 15 —

We waited for Jules by the front door. Mel flicked a piece of cat shit at the corner with the toe of her boot. "You'd think it'd shit in its box."

"The old man said it was lonely, cause its kitten's dead and it's old."

"Yeah? I bet Mom gets pretty lonely too, but you don't see her shitting in the hall."

The old woman stood up and walked over to us. "Happy now?" she shot out.

Mel ignored her. "He had to put my knees up to my chest to get it in, it was so big," Mel said to me and smiled, her eyes huge.

The old woman shook her head. "I've been you. I've been you and it's taken me a hell of a long time to get over it."

"What's her problem?" Mel asked, picking at blisters in the smoke-washed wallpaper.

I looked at the old woman and tried to figure it out. She was haggard looking, worn out. She was a hundred years old, if forty, and she lived in a house that smelt of cat piss. *That* was her problem.

"Forget it," I said, and pulled Mel out the door.

Only the old woman didn't leave. Instead, she shut the storm door behind us, and crossed her arms, watching us as if we might steal the light bulb overhead. Stamping my feet against the cold, I resigned myself to waiting for Jules and Darryl outside.

Mel turned to me and said, "You and Darryl, huh? What's Woody gonna say?"

"Nothing," I said, "since you're not going to say nothing to the Woodsman since there's nothing to say. Besides, it wouldn't matter if you did, since me and him are only friends and he's still in love with you. But don't, okay? It's embarrassing."

"Really?" Mel scavenged her purse for the glasses.

"Yeah, I mean, Darryl's sort of, I don't know, he's *Darryl*."

"No, Woody's still into me?"

I nodded, miserable.

"I thought you and him would've gotten together by now, for sure," she said.

"No." I scraped at the bricks with my finger-nail. "He's sort of funny."

"You use a condom?" Thick lenses in place once more, Mel's eyes grew large.

"Yeah, mostly," I said quietly. I was conscious of the old woman, who wasn't pretending not to listen, "but it made his dick look weird, and it busted and he was all like, *well, hell*. And I guess, we, you know, we kept on doing it."

"Didn't Ronnie teach you nothing?" Mel asked, squinting her eyes.

I shrugged and looked over the woman's narrow shoulder, wondering where Darryl was now. He'd evaporated after we were done. I pictured his face, twitching one moment and relaxed into Zen-like composure the next.

"Don't say anything to anybody, okay?"

Mel scraped the ash off her smoke with her long pinky nail and I knew she'd keep quiet.

As the wind picked up, I could hear small snapping sounds from the trees around us. It was the same sound my knee was making as I stamped off the cold. In camp, they'd made us take orienteering, so we wouldn't lose ourselves in the trees. There, Mr. Yu introduced us to the sound of stress fractures. Tiny little breaks inside of each branch that were meant to keep the whole limb from downing in the wind.

Mr. Yu asked us to hold our arms out like the branches of a tree and described the series of tiny fractures we would soon undergo as a gift. I mean, he said that. He *actually* said that. Mr. Yu moved through the group of tree-children at Camp Totoredaka, set our limbs swaying, and mirroring our movements, he'd said, "these tiny fractures you hear are a gift: over time, they're what keep us from breaking entirely," and our round faces looked up at him with troubled wonder.

"I think I might've screwed up," I said, meaning everything. My entire life, basically.

"It gets better," Mel assured me.

"How would you know?" I asked, and she let out a guffaw.

Stepping outside, the woman grasped Mel's shoulder from behind and said, "I *was* you," and leaning in to Mel's shoulder, she said it again, "I was just like you."

"Don't flatter yourself," Mel said, shaking the woman off.

When my sister swung round to face the woman, her hands were shaking. The woman, by comparison, looked calm, almost indifferent.

Mel looked the old woman over. "You might want to try doing something with yourself," she said, "I mean, you can't always have been so ... used up."

The old woman squinted and spat on the ground at Mel's feet.

"Holy fuck," Mel said, "did you see that? Jesus, I was trying to help the old lady out."

"Enough," Jules said, stepping outside. He gave Mel a warning look.

The old woman sucked her teeth and Jules,

he took hold of Mel's hand, pulling her down the drive.

On the stoop, I mumbled an apology.

The old woman looked me in the eyes for the first time that night and said, "If you're not careful, you'll end up the same, like that one," and went back into the house. At that, she closed the front door, shutting out the last square of light in the universe.

The stars were dim and the night was that scary kind of quiet that creeps up on characters in a horror flick before the killing begins. It was the first time I'd been struck by how isolated the house was. Out in the middle of nowhere, outside of Streetsville, up the lonely part of Queen. I was scared of the horrors I'd seen projected on the screen each two-dollar Tuesday for the whole of my life. I knew the golden rule of slasher flicks: the girl who does it, gets it. Only now, that girl was me.

By the car, Jules danced Mel around to the passenger's side and pinned her against the door and she gave out a little yelp.

He pulled Mel close, by the shoulders, and gently asked, "You hurt?"

"Yeah, my back hurts like a bitch," Mel said.

"That's not what I meant."

"I know what you meant," and feeling for

the edges of the bandage, she said, "It's not so bad. Just a little prick."

Jules let go of Mel, but maybe pushed a little too, because she fell back against the car door. And right away he raised his open palms in the air to show that he'd never touched a thing in his life. Shaking his head, Jules walked around to the driver's side, slamming the door when he got in. After taking a deep breath, Mel got in the Volvo too, sitting down gingerly as if the tattoo pained her.

A couple seconds passed.

"Tell her to get in the car," Jules said.

He was revving the engine like a maniac. I didn't want to get in.

"Get in the car," Mel said, mimicking Jules.

I smirked and fished in my purse for a cigarette. It was true, I was wasting time. I wanted Darryl to come and say good night. In my head, it was important to work out if we were *lovers*, like in a Zeffirelli film. I knew that *Endless Love* was total bullshit, and nothing meant anything, and besides, in the film, David burned down Jade's house, which was seriously fucked, and while in no way did I want Darryl to burn down my house, even if it was a rental, I did want him to reappear momentarily, like condensation when a room has cooled. Of course, my grades were pretty borderline in science.

"Get in the car or you're staying," Jules told

me.

"You better get in the car," said Mel.

I opened the back door and slid in, pressing the back of my head against the car seat. But the car didn't move. In a tired voice, Mel said, "I meant the tattoo, all right Jules, I was talking about the goddamned tattoo. And it was a joke, anyways. Just a stupid joke."

There was an edge to Mel's voice. Something was bothering her. Something more than what had happened with her and Jules. I think the old woman had gotten to her.

Jules nodded and leaned across the stick shift and something put me on edge.

"I can't talk to you with those things on your face," he said.

Mel stared past the windshield for a long time before taking off her glasses. When she did take them off, Jules leaned in and took my sister's face into his hands. It was one of those sudden kisses that you're never ready for and when he let go, the back of Mel's head hit the passenger window. She'd been trying to pull away.

"Dick," I said.

Mel fixed her gaze on the windshield and Jules turned to look at me. I knew better than to say anything, even "sorry." I slowly scraped the ash from my cigarette and waited him out.

The first time the Woodsman came to our place Mom set out all these snacks for people because it was Christmas Eve, and the Woodsman, who had stringy black hair hanging to one side of his face, had taken a bite of one sandwich and then another, throwing them back on the pile after tasting each, and Mom's face hardened and you could tell she wanted to toss him, but didn't, because it was Christmas and, punk or no, he was Mel's boyfriend, and though he knew better, he was too screwed up to pay attention to what Mom called *the little voice*, and I think Mom somehow guessed that telling a greasy kid to listen to the *little voice inside of him* wasn't going to go over so hot, though who knows, it might have, because the Woodsman could surprise you. Seriously, though, if you'd been a beaten kid, like the Woodsman, and our Mom heard about it, she'd pretty much feel sympathy for you no matter what you got up to. It almost made me wish *I'd* been beaten, though I suppose *that* wouldn't count since Mom would figure I deserved the beating if she was the one who gave it. After he left the kitchen, Mom salvaged the sandwiches, cutting around the bite-holes, so she could eat them herself. By the next Christmas, she had the Woodsman paper-trained, as she put it. He got up and got Mom her sandwiches and took care in arranging them on the plate. And he remembered to give her a napkin, to boot.

Long story short, there was something wrong with how Jules kissed Mel. It hadn't been a kiss so much as a hole Jules was making where her mouth had been. I wondered whether Mel would ever paper-train Jules.

Jules was still staring at me in silence. "Leave it," Mel said to him, and glanced at me. "Let's go already. Drop her at Ronnie's and we can talk."

Her voice sounded odd, and I couldn't tell if she was about to cry or cuss him out.

"Please," she added.

That's when I knew she was about to cry. Mel *never* said please.

Jules put the car in reverse and backed out of the driveway killer fast. The rest of the ride was quiet. Dead quiet. Nobody bothered to put the radio on.

Ten minutes later, we pulled up.

I got out and Mel started to get out with me, but Jules grabbed her hand and looked up at her, just looked, and that was it. She sat back down, sadder than ever.

I walked up to Ronnie's window and clinked my nails along the glass. The lights were out and I rapped a little harder, but still, nothing. Finally,

I lay on the lawn to watch each breath emerge from my mouth. Now that I was alone, the sensations in my body competed for attention: the shrilling pain at the small of my back, where the old man's needle had made a thousand or more tiny incisions, leaving an inky residue, mixed with blood, and a dull burning pain between my legs that I wasn't ready to think about. I thought to myself, that's how it is with the kind of rooms that make you a stranger to yourself. It's okay when you're inside of them, you make sense, but coming home alongside the other person you've been is hard sometimes.

My first time had been okay, I suppose, only I'd always thought it would come with a gradually swelling soundtrack and that the bruises on my legs would fade. Okay, maybe not so dramatic as that, but I hadn't imagined sloshy sounds and clicking teeth over a scratchy track by Sammy Hagar, which he'd put on specifically, *first* the Hagar and *then* the condom, and while I'd known it'd hurt, I hadn't imagined the pain as real. I wasn't sure, but I suspected that the sex had been ordinary, and ordinary, I was willing to bet, is better with someone who likes you. Like, say, the Woodsman. I mean, if he wanted me around after this one.

Right then, I knew I had to do it at least one more time in my life, if only so that the second time could bleed over the memory of the first, and make it feel less second-hand.

I kept looking to see the Woodsman walking up the street, as impossible as that was. Lying on my back, I turned my ear to the ground and listened for footsteps, hearing instead Mel and Jules as they had it out, voices nearly indistinguishable over the engine's rough idle.

After twenty minutes, the Volvo pulled away from the curb and Mel scooched in beside me and I felt better, because I didn't want to be all alone with my thoughts right then, and we looked up at the night sky and for the longest time, we didn't say a thing.

- 16 -

Cassette tape. December 1975

Karin: Okay, there we go. It's on now, I think.
        Yeah okay, do you want to, uh, tell me
        what, what you did today?

Mel: Nothin'.

Lora: No-oo. We played, we played at the
        park.

Karin: Yeah, that's right, sweetie, you went out
        to play, you went out to play at the park.
        And what happened there, what did you
        see there at the park?

Mel: The birds, Mommy?

Karin: Yeah, sweetie, tell about the birds again.

Mel: We saved them.

Lora: Poof!

Karin: You saved them?

Mel: Mmhmm.

Karin: Tell me how you, what were they doing when, when you found them.

Mel: We went to the park and we was walking and ... and we just saw them, that's all, when we was walking.

Lora: There, Mommy, there.

Karin: On the ground? You found them on the ground?

Mel: Yep.

Lora: Uh-huh.

Karin: And how were the birds, what were they like when you found them?

Lora: Like this, they were like this.

Mel: Because they froze, their wings were froze.

Lora: They froze that way, cause I know why. Cause they curl up to sleep. Cause it gets very, very cold. Cause they are sleepy. And the rain gets 'em.

Karin: And what did you do to the birds?

Mel: We warmed them, Mommy. We holded them in our mitts –

Lora: Yeah! Yeah! And then we had to, we we blowed, then poof!

Karin: Poof?

Lora: Like this, it flies, poof, it flies out my mittens! And then –

Mel: No, we melted the wings, like this, Mommy. Hoo-hoo-hoo. And *then* the birds, they got warm and then –

Lora: They flied –

Mel: – and they go up up up.

Lora: They flied out of our mittens!

Mel: We breathed on them and then they flied away.

− 17 −
Lora

"Do you think anything lives out there," I asked, staring at a reddish star.

Mel thought about it for a second. "Yeah," she said, "I do."

"Really, you do?"

"Yep."

"Like aliens?"

"Yeah, small and stupid ones, the size of amoebas, and if they come, by accident, they're going to mistake people for planets and then we'll all be totally fucked."

I shifted to my side and looked at Mel. Sometimes it was hard to know what was going on in her head. She could say the weirdest things.

"No, seriously."

"Seriously? I don't think there's anything out there, except maybe that, Martian germs or something. People are freaks. A total accident. And till we blot ourselves out, we're all we've got. Take that star," she said, picking a bright one, "the light takes so long to travel here, it looks like there's something on fire up there, but there's not. There's nothing. The stars could all have been dead for a thousand years."

"They can't *all* be dead."

"They could be, seriously, but probably not. And there are new stars, ones whose light we can't see, in places that look dead to us now. See there? That one's Venus and that one's Mars. And those," she said, pointing to a cluster, "those are the sisters."

"Oh hey, I took your picture," I said, pulling the Polaroid out of my purse.

"Cool. Where're the rest?"

"They got burned."

"Oh man, why didn't you burn this one? It's *so* lame."

"But you're a virgin in that one." I pulled out my compact and held it up to her. "See, you can hold it up to a mirror like this and see if anything's different. Like if you've changed."

"Like if I've sprouted a third eye."

"No. Something's gotta be different, though, right?"

Mel took the compact from me and patted beige powder over her forehead and nose.

"Yeah, something's different all right," she

said.

"No, I mean, maybe you look more *worldly*."

"That wasn't my first time, Lora, just the first time I did it with Jules."

"Oh."

"No biggie. I'm not sure I like him."

I lay on my side, facing Mel.

"I wish I'd never met Darryl," I said, "I mean, I thought he'd be different."

Mel propped herself up on her elbow and waited.

"I guess it's all fine since I wanted to get it over with and now it's done and I won't die a virgin and I don't know, maybe it'll all work out okay in the end, even. You know, with Darryl. I mean, now that we're *lovers* and everything."

Mel picked at the grass, her voice serious. "Look, I know this is new to you, but if you want my advice, don't get too attached. There's no point. There's like less than no point."

"I know."

Mel tucked a strand of hair behind my ear and asked me for the second time, "You okay, kiddo?"

"Fine," I said, shaking the hair loose. "I don't care. I thought he was different, that's all."

"I'll give you this, you're braver than me," she said. "Hey, you try the window?"

"No, I thought I'd lie out here in the fucking cold because I want to freeze my ass off."

"You know," she said, "we should all get sterilized, every last one of us should get our tubes tied or our 'nads cut off and then we could all die out and leave the planet to the fucking animals." Pulling a mickey of rum from her jacket, she added, "Here, have some, it'll make you warm."

"You stole from Jules?"

"No, I got it given to me." After digging around in her purse, Mel tossed a pack my way, "here, you can have these, too," and pulling the plastic from a second pack, she added, "Jules is always visiting home and giving me shit. He's not so bad. I mean, when he's not being a dick."

"They're brown."

"Off brand," she said with authority. "They're good for you. It means you're not smoking bleach for a change." Mel passed the bottle and tapped her cigarette against the pack, tamping down the tobacco, a habit she'd picked up from Jules.

"Look," she said, "You *are* brave. Me, I'd never do it with a guy who wasn't halfway in love with me. The secret is, when a guy's in love, he's sort of blind, you know. He doesn't see anything, he doesn't see what's wrong with you. It's like all the lights in the world go out. All the stars die at once when you do it. But some guy, some random guy, I don't know, that's like doing it in the doctor's office, the lights are *so* on, and I think that's brave, you know. I mean, in a way, it's brave."

"Really?"

"Well, yeah, maybe that's one way to look at it."

"How did you get Jules to like you?"

"I didn't have to *get* him to," Mel said, rolling her eyes.

"Okay, so then how did you get Mikey to like you, pray tell? Or Jason. Or Lee. I mean, how is it that every boy in the entire world likes you?"

I paused.

"Even fish boy likes you," I added.

Mel looked at me, her fingers touching her mouth. She knew exactly who I meant.

"You mean Woody," she asked quietly.

I nodded. Val had started calling the Woodsman "fish boy" when he got a part-time job at the fish and chips place at South Common Mall.

"You're thinking about Woody, still?" she asked softly.

"Yeah, well, maybe I'm the patron saint of fish boys," I said.

Mel guffawed and I waited, but she had nothing more to say. I wanted to press her, only the lights came on, Ronnie and Val opened the window, and I never got to hear how it was boys liked Mel.

I woke alone on the floor next to Ronnie's bed. It was the middle of the night and Mel was gone. The Baxters' cat, a calico named Spot, had curled into my legs for warmth, and when I sat up, she hissed and recoiled as if the furniture had betrayed her.

I could hear Mr. Baxter in the living room. You'd find him there, when he was to be found at all, sitting on the couch and sounding off like some kind of a war vet, though I never asked which war, and so far as I know, Canada wasn't in Vietnam. Garry Baxter was mythical to Mel, seeing as he'd known our father since they were both fourteen. Only problem being, no matter how deft Mel's efforts at uncovering information, Garry Baxter shook his head, raised an eyebrow and, drinking or not, looked at us as if to say, do you really think I'd fall for that?

Garry Baxter was the only one any of us knew who'd been to university, besides Nanna, but while Nanna would glow if either of us asked about her *university years*, as she called them, Mr. Baxter soured. Cathy told us he'd only gone for two and a half months, so I guess it was his *university weeks* Mr. Baxter hadn't enjoyed.

There were a number of subjects not to be brought up in Mr. Baxter's presence. The problem being there was no master list and I never knew what was the next wrong thing to say. Take the time I'd asked about the seat belts. You wouldn't think seat belts were controversial and all I wanted to know was how a tiny strap could do any good, seeing as it hung so loose around the torso.

Without answering, Mr. Baxter floored the gas. When the car was going at a good clip, he slammed on the brakes and yanked the steering wheel side to side, sending the car careening between shoulders as it criss-crossed a solid yellow line. I bounced around in the back some, but Mel was braced by the belt in the front, which instantly tightened and held her in place, like a caterpillar in a straightjacket cocoon.

In the living room, Val Swynerchuk reached for a third slice of pizza, and Mr. Baxter looked at her for a long time, like he'd only just noticed that Val existed. And he leaned over to my sister and, indicating Val with his chin, told Mel there were two kinds of people. Those who give off energy, an aura, and psychic vampires who drain the energy of others.

"So, which one's she?" Mel asked.

Val plopped herself back on the couch, sullenly picked the mushrooms off her slice and winged them at the box's lid. Staring at her as he spoke, Mr. Baxter said "I'll tell you what that one does. She sucks it up. She sucks the last bit of juice from everyone around her to survive."

Turning to Mel again, he said, "But I didn't have to look at her to tell you that."

Swynerchuk made a face, and threw another mushroom. This one landed on the carpet in a skid of tomato sauce and cheese.

Mr. Baxter liked my sister and so it didn't occur to her to worry about what he'd make of her. And maybe it *was* true about Val. She *was* awfully good at getting people to do stuff for her, whether she liked them or not. Only there'd been circumstances that had forced her to develop that particular talent, and I wouldn't have wanted to be the one to point it out.

- 19 -

The half-empty mickey of rum was on the table in front of my sister, Val had nodded off on the chair and Ronnie's Mom, Cathy, was nowhere in sight. Mr. Baxter leaned forward, looking at Mel. It was the kind of look that would have made me squirm. Mr. Baxter calmly looked into your eyes and spoke in what would have been a reassuring voice if you didn't associate the tone with veterinarians, who used a similar soft pitch in their approach to injured animals. It was three in the morning, and Mr. Baxter wanted to know what part of the body was most important when it came to sex.

Val began to snore and Ronnie rolled her eyes. She walked into the kitchen, turned on the radio and filled the kettle with water. Mel may have been her best friend, but as soon as Mr. Baxter got started on one of his tangents, nothing in this world could convince her to endure it. For my part, I found Mr. Baxter's question interesting and, while Ronnie got out the teapot, I stood in the kitchen doorway and picked at air bubbles and loose paint on the door frame.

"Well, there's the obvious ones," Mel said, listing the polite glossary of sex organs we'd memorized in health class. Mel sounded bored. She picked at the threadbare arm of the couch as she answered.

Mr. Baxter's brown hair was thinning at the top and you could see a hint of the bone structure under his skin. He was lean, the opposite of Ronnie's Mom, and he was oddly attractive too. It was hard to see how Cathy and Mr. Baxter could have gotten together and harder to see, at times like this, why they were still together. Mr. Baxter was skinny, but he wasn't frail or weak. Mr. Baxter was skinny and tough-looking, but elegant too. After three drinks, he forgot that he was supposed to be somebody's dad and talked like a normal person. One who'd never had kids and so, hadn't learned to act fake. He'd been *places*. He'd done *things*.

As exciting as Mr. Baxter was, over us loomed the constant threat of being revealed as the idiot he'd always suspected you to be. And you'd never know it beforehand. No, he'd pick up on it *for* you, in something you'd always and unaccountably held to be normal, and so had never guessed was out and out retarded, at least, not until he let you in on it. It was a gift Mr. Baxter had, a genuine talent. Which explained a lot about Ronnie, who'd always been solid, but tended to hide any qualities she might have under a flat line.

Mel had given a dozen suggestions that ranged from the obvious to more imaginative entries, like "curled index finger." She'd be slapstick one second and flatly intoning in the dead language of *Health & Guidance* the next. I looked at Mr. Baxter skeptically. Mel's list was exhaustive. I didn't think there was a part of the human body she hadn't named. If a body part could be stuck in something or have something stuck into it, it made her list. With each entry, she plucked a piece of fuzz off of the arm of the chair and dropped it into a growing pile.

Without looking up, Mel said, "I've got it. The mouth." She was smiling like someone had handed her a gun.

My sister, with a smile I'd never seen, slowly levelled her gaze at Mr. Baxter. Leaning forward, she said in a steady voice, "Some men, Mr. Baxter, like it in the mouth. Is that what you like? Do you like a girl to take it in the mouth?" She cocked her head and raised an eyebrow.

Mr. Baxter smiled, shook his head, and said, "Not the point."

"I give," she said, levelling the little pile of lint as she flopped back on the threadworn La-Z-Boy.

Mr. Baxter pointed at his head with a skinny finger. His hand looked like a gun.

"The brain."

Mel looked at him skeptically.

"The biggest sex organ in the human body is the brain," he repeated, pouring himself another glass of rum and staining it with Coke.

I considered what was for me a revelation: the human brain. Until that second, it hadn't occurred to me that the human brain was involved in sex. Which might be why things hadn't gone perfectly with Darryl. I hadn't made use of the human brain. I pictured him after, when he'd sat on the mattress with his back to me, small shivers running down his spine, naked except for socks which were of two different colours and lengths.

Mel scoffed and reached for the rum, but Mr. Baxter was faster. He placed the flat of his hand across the bottle's opening, and shook his head. "Nice try," he said.

Mel slowly sat back on the worn chair.

Gesturing with his rocks glass, Mr. Baxter said, "I wouldn't expect you girls to know much about *good* sex," and made an expansive gesture which included me. "You're both young and young people don't know what they've got. That's the real paradox with girls. I mean, look at you. You've been given these young, beautiful bodies, and on the inside, you're all keyed up," he said, "but it won't be until you're a little older that you'll know what to do with what you've got, and by then, well, by then you won't be nearly so young or so beautiful."

Mr. Baxter spoke of our bodies' inevitable decay with an ease that was shocking.

"Funny," Mel said, settling her behind into the chair, "because I seem to manage."

Mr. Baxter laughed.

"Oh, sure, you can do it," he said. "You don't have to be a genius to spread your legs. But can you get and give *real* pleasure? Not in the way I mean. Your biggest sex organ, your brain, won't be fully developed for a few more years. Five years from now, then, then you might have something to talk about. But it won't be until you're thirty that you'll have the real hang of sex. And by then," he said, "well, by then it won't be nearly so pretty."

Mr. Baxter looked up as Cathy walked into the room and took her chair. Their place was small, the bathroom and kitchen just off the tiny living room, and the smells crept in, one after another, but everyone pretended to ignore the stink of fish and grease and shit. Cathy picked up the newspaper and a pencil and started in on a crossword puzzle. In the kitchen, Ronnie heaved herself up onto the counter, and tucked her shirt under her breasts. She squeezed a little Vaseline into her hands and rubbed the swell of her belly. She was, as both our moms put it, *five months gone*. The way our mothers talked, you'd think that at the moment of impact between sperm and egg, Ronnie had vacated the premises, giving her body up to the unborn or else, more likely, their stubborn directives. I leaned in and took a closer look.

"Still an innie, huh?"

"Yup," she said.

"It's a little bit less of an innie, maybe," I said.

Ronnie shrugged, "It's the same."

"Yeah, I guess. But maybe it's a little more out than yesterday."

I turned back to the living room. Cathy was gnawing the ass end of a pencil. Though her body was soft, like a generous sofa, there was an underlying stiffness to her posture. When Mr. Baxter was away, it was Cathy's house and laughter percolated throughout the rooms. But when Mr. Baxter was around, not only did Cathy's stomach problems return, but Ronnie was somehow smaller, taking up hardly any space at all. She'd hover in the background, like a moth trapped under a drinking glass. I guess it balanced out in the end since Mr. Baxter was hardly ever home. Maybe if he was around, taking up space more often, he wouldn't have had to make everyone around him feel so small.

Mr. Baxter started talking about his red-headed girlfriend and Mel, she started to amass a new pile of lint.

"A *real* red-head," he yawned, "if you know what I mean." Mr. Baxter glanced at Cathy, whose soft orange hair had never looked so unnaturally even in tone as it did now. Her hair was the colour of a knitted scarf I'd bought at the Biway, only to get it outside and see how crass the colour was in the light of day.

I heard a crash and Ronnie cursing. In the kitchen, something was newly broken.

"Wanna take out the garbage?" I asked, tapping two fingers against my lips.

Ronnie nodded.

I tossed the shards into the half empty Glad bag and tied it off while Ronnie grabbed us a couple coats. She tossed one to me.

— 20 —

Letter, September 21, 1984

Dear Mel,

I feel things I can't talk to anybody about, sometimes I know my baby is dreaming inside of me
and sometimes, I feel you, you're in the room
with me, I'm getting ready to go out and I feel
you floating over me, I look in the mirror and
it's like you're looking at me and telling me I got
it right, smiling on us, looking over us, seeing
the baby sleeping inside of me, you're smiling
and I get the idea that you're happier now than
you used to be, that you're okay now, can you
please somehow let me know?

Ronnie

— 21 —

Lora

While Ronnie fussed with the garbage cans, raccoons had been and gone, I stood and waited at
the side of the house, next to the woodpile.
Under Mr. Baxter's warm parka, I had on an
oversize T-shirt, and my blood was flecked with
crystals of ice. After weighing the lids down
with rocks, Ronnie came and stood next to me.
She looked like shit.

"I need a fucking job," I said before she had
a chance. Ronnie eyed me warily and pulled two
cigarettes out of her pack, holding one out to
me.

"Mrs. Penchuk will probably hire me this
summer," I told her.

I'd been a *mother's helper* for Mrs. Penchuk
the summer before, but she hadn't called me
back about this summer. Perhaps because the
last time, I'd broken a vase and when I told her,

she put on the expression she usually reserved for her dog, Barkley, those times he shat on the shag, the long, woolly stuff that grew out of their bedroom floor like a 1970s nightmare. She had two little kids, girls, and I was glad of that. Little boys throw rocks and if you ask why, they look at you like they have no clue what you're on about. I decided to call Mrs. Penchuk in the morning, in case their answering machine was broken or she'd lost my number or forgotten who I was.

"I found this old ratty paperback full of ideas at the swap meet," I told Ronnie, "like take old macaroni and glue and aluminum pie plates, ribbon and paint, and make party hats. I'm so full of ideas, she'll probably take me back. Plus, it pays sixty a week. Which I need. And maybe more cause I'm a year older."

Ronnie hunched down into her shoulders, and nodded.

"Mr. Penchuk isn't around much. He's like hardly *ever* there," I added. "Which is why she needs me." I sort of rambled on about how they had a nice house, the nicest I'd seen, and listed off the kind of stuff they left lying around in the yard and wouldn't miss.

But for some reason, my thoughts kept returning to Mr. Donald, who lived a few units down from us. I'd babysat for him too, on occasion, watching his two little boys. One night,

Mel joined me and we'd gone through all of the drawers in his study, discovering his stash of porn. Only the pictures were of little boys like his own. One of the boys wore a costume. He stood in front of a cement wall in a cowboy hat, vinyl belt and plastic holster, but he had no clothes. And there was this funny little expression on his upturned face as if he was wondering whether or not he was in trouble. Mel and I didn't talk about what we saw in those magazines. We looked at the pictures in silence and then put them back. Mel was unnaturally quiet. Before Mr. Donald could return, she made an excuse and left.

While I stood on the front porch and waited to be paid, Mr. Donald paused, the money in his hand, and searched my expression. I couldn't look him in the face. I stared at the bricks and finally, looked down, holding my hand out. He tossed the bills on the ground and quietly shut the door. A moment later, the light in his study came on.

I kept waiting for someone to take him away, but the next summer, there he was, out in the sun with his garden hose, spraying the co-op boys with water. Everything blurred together in my head. When his thinning Lycra got wet, I thought it would erode like wet paper.

"I was thinking, you know, about that old guy four doors down," I said, butting the smoke on my heel, "remember, the one with the weird chest."

"Uh, no."

"The guy in the complex who's so bony. Remember?"

Ronnie shook her head.

"Mr. Donald," I said.

Ronnie looked at me like I was nuts, "That guy's a fucking perv," she said, and butted her smoke on the asphalt. "What are you doing thinking about him, anyway."

I shrugged. Took another drag. "Your dad is kind of fucked, eh?"

"One of these days I'm going to find my *real* dad," she said.

"He ever write you back?"

"I don't think the letters get through his people. I have to find a way to see him. At a gig or something." Ronnie lit up a second smoke and blew a perfect smoke ring. A second and third pierced the first. "You ever think about finding yours?" she asked.

"I don't know. I guess I could. Mel talks about it."

"We should do it together," Ronnie said. She was excited by the idea, the only problem being that Mr. Baxter *was* Ronnie's real dad.

"Yeah, maybe," I said, "but then, maybe let's

not, too. Can I check again?"

"Just for a sec," Ronnie said, unzipping her coat, "it's frickin' cold out."

Ronnie took another drag as I reached into her jacket and touched the round swell. It was amazing and soft and warm under there and I loved it when the baby kicked me. Every once in a while, I liked to reach in and tap a little with my index finger. I'd do it gently, the way you'd tap on the glass side of a fish tank, so as to alert but not shock the fish inside. I didn't want to miss the times where the baby notices and kicks back. Ronnie passed me the tail end of her cig, zipped back up and headed inside.

After taking it down to the filter, I launched the butt with my thumb and forefinger. It went sailing all the way to the base of the drive. I could cut a good arc with a cigarette butt and was pretty proud. I caught up with Ronnie inside the door.

"Don't you wish we could keep her?"

Ronnie didn't say anything, but she looked miserable and I could tell she both wished we could and would either punch me or bawl if I said another word. Then the zipper on Mr. Baxter's fur-lined parka jammed with me inside and it took my full concentration just to line up the little metal teeth and get free.

— 22 —

Karin

You don't know. Not until it happens. You can't trust anyone. People talk. They talk about what happened. They talk about you. Try to make sense of things. And there you are in the thick of it. And what, people believe, keeps their own kids safe is this one fact: *They're* not *you*.

They find comfort in thinking the worst of you. Honest to God.

Human nature.

It's not pretty, but that's what it is: *human nature*. Animals don't disappoint. They do what's natural. It's people who are unnatural. People disappoint.

The police believed my girl ran away. When they finally started looking, it was at Mel's young man. He was sad. Genuinely. Not a bad kid, I'd say, not like they made him out. I wouldn't even say he qualified as a screw-up. He's turned things around this last year. Got himself a decent job. And he's kept it a while, now, too.

What I know is this:

She wasn't in her bed when I left for work. That happens. Happens all the time. Lora will sleep late and Mel will catch the bus without her. That afternoon, Lora calls me at work and I learn that Mel hasn't been at school. Not that day. A bad feeling came over me. A *this is it* kind of feeling.

It isn't until the next afternoon that the call comes in. The cleaning staff have found her knapsack at Islington station. Her knapsack, her boots. Her ID. That bad feeling takes root. Like a cancer. I know something is wrong. I *know*.

My daughter is not a runaway. And if she is, it doesn't matter how she got out. Once she was out there, it went bad.

So I collect her things. From the subway station. The sun is giving off a cold grey light. I see it still. The exact quality of light that day. Strange. Dead and grey. It lights up the surfaces of things, but dulls them too.

The knapsack is heavy. Strangely heavy. Makes me wonder if she carries rocks in there.

— 23 —
Lora

There's normal and then there's normal. The new version goes like this: Since Mel's been gone, which means for now and probably forever, it's me and it's Mom. We take care of ourselves and we take care of each other. Nobody else counts, not when it comes down to it. Other people can be figured in, temporarily, like an extra pork chop at dinner time or a new dress for Mom, but that doesn't change how we sum things up. It's me and it's Mom. We take care of ourselves. Period.

The second time Mel ran away, the Woodsman came over and we sat him in Mel's place for dinner and Uncle Dave, he looked at the Woodsman, waving a pork chop on the end of his fork, and said, "Lora's never needed anybody in her life and she's not going to start now, so don't be getting any big ideas."

Ideas, he says, his mouth in a smirk, and the word sounds so dirty it stinks.

I guess not needing anyone makes me feel proud, but it's scary too. Deep down, I know it's true, I *don't* need anybody, but when he says it, I think of the story Mom used to tell us when we were kids, the one about the little lost star. The one Mom stopped telling us, along with *The Little Match Girl*, because both of those fairy tales can give a kid some serious nightmares. In the story, the little star is Katika, she's the flowerpot girl, and her whole world is a flowerpot, the earth has vanished from beneath her feet, and she is holding onto the upside-down pot with both of her hands, sitting there forever, spinning off through the universe all alone in the dark. For the life of me, I can't remember how she got there and I guess it doesn't matter. All I know is that I don't want to be that girl. But then, I don't think we get much choice over who we are.

"It's better to have something you don't need, than need something you don't have," is what my Uncle Dave always says, and I guess that makes my sister a gun. Only Uncle Dave is always saying one thing is just like another and when it comes down to it, I know that nothing is like any other thing.

− 24 −

Mom used to fit into my theory. That is, when we went into rooms that made us strangers to ourselves *and* came out of them as well. Mom was the place we'd come home to after, when we were done with such rooms or they were done with us. We'd come home and the places we'd been and what they'd made of us would become remote and surreal. Mom knew us that well. I'd come home and camp out on the couch beside her and she'd press the palm of her hand against my forehead, as if I might have caught a fever out there, and instantly, I'd be the same person I'd been as a little kid. It always amazes me to feel that small and young inside. All because Mom cares about how things come out for us in the end. Which isn't true of most of the places a kid happens to find herself in.

The biggest difference between Mom and those other places is that she loves us. I never doubt that. I don't doubt it, now, even if a dull glaze collects over her eyes at night and there's a sadness to her that nothing can shake. Nowadays, when I camp out on the couch beside her, it's me looking to see if her chin has slipped down over her chest, to measure the weight of her head, tipping down, as she nods off. That's how I know it's time to pack her up the stairs to bed.

Every night it's the same story. She comes in from work and I put dinner on the stove and while pale noodles solidify at the bottom of her bowl, she pours herself the first of three or four rye and Cokes, and she sips and stares at the tube and if I'm in a talkative mood, if the doorbell doesn't ring, if Fred Irving doesn't come to stay the night, I'll tell her how my day went during a commercial. It's my old idea of perfect, how she doesn't get mad at anything I do, not even my grades. So long as there are reruns of *Love Boat* on the tube and rye in the cupboard and a few cans of Coke, and so long as there's bread to toast and peanut butter in the jar, so long as there's a pack of smokes in the freezer, we're doing okay.

These days, Mom is in her own world, and there's "private" written on the door and "do not disturb" hanging from the knob, and there's nothing to be done about it. I get the feeling that if I could picture us as a happy family, if I could picture us doing well, that would be enough. Only all of my pictures of us have a hole in the middle where Mel should be.

Part Two

— I —
Lora

In some ways, it wasn't Mel who was gone, it was everyone who hadn't loved her that was gone. After Mel, my field of vision became unstable. I became prone to drift. In all things. It was an effort, a real effort, to focus in and talk to people. The ones I clung to were Mom and Uncle Dave, Val and the Woodsman.

The world that went on without Mel in it became dim. I could list the things that were real to me on one hand. Mel's old glasses were real, and so were the people I could see with the glasses, the signs of hurt eaten into, made soft, by her powerful lens.

Nobody and nothing else mattered.

When I missed her badly enough, I could put on the glasses and we could look out at the world together. I could sense her, the moment I stopped seeing everything clearly and my world clouded up like hers would when she would take her glasses off each night before slipping into bed.

After she was gone, my sister and I were more alike than ever. We shared the same lens and we shared the same language. My experiences did not happen apart from her. I could not, in my head, split off from Mel because she was gone. To think about Mel meant my experiences, even those without her, were bound up with her still.

I began to remember events in my life in the words I would choose to talk to Mel about them. The shortcuts I'd take, the signposts we shared, the language we spoke. Everything was happening in a way that Melissa would understand and no one else. I guess the frame you bring to any experience is as important as the experience itself. Everything that happens now happens in a way only Mel would get. And for the most part, anything our language can't hold dissolves, leaving the event simpler, without so many incongruous edges. Everything that happens to me now is of a piece with Melissa, the Melissa who lost her acuity of vision, the Melissa who, at the very last, lost her glasses too.

Our bodies are alike. You could once tell us apart because she was half an inch taller and wore glasses. Since she's been gone, I sometimes wear glasses too. I've grown since then, filled out, and so our identities come down to the difference between our two tattoos. To who displays the rich tones of a breaking chrysalis, and who, in prison-blue ink, bears the mark of what must appear to be, to a stranger's eyes, the smallest and most ordinary of doors.

— 2 —

Everything has a beginning. My sister's disappearance has to have one. There has to be a time, a moment, in which she began to disappear.

I've looked for some sign that Mel was poised to leave. Maybe it was there in the world she saw around us, the one that was slowly dying as we pretended not to see. Or in her dreams of the A-bomb, quietly imploding in our mouths as we slept, shattering millions on millions of teeth. A city's worth of polished bone, demolished in an instant. And what could any of us do but stir in our sleep, lick at broken mouths, and feel ourselves already dead, this as the fire consumed the part of us that could dream of bombs to begin with.

Or maybe the beginning was obvious. Like they say.

Maybe it was there for all to see.

Maybe it did begin, as the police insisted

those first days she was gone, in my sister's previous attempts at running. Or maybe, as our neighbour sees it, it all began with an awful trip to the hospital the weekend before Mel vanished, when the nurse, Mrs. Nowlan from Unit 137, nullified the contents of a fifteen-year-old girl's stomach with activated charcoal, this after sliding a tube into Mel's nose that, as my sister quietly choked it down, snaked the full length of her esophagus, pumping close to a bottle of aspirin out of her, depositing it into a large silver bowl they'd balanced on her lap. Mom and me watched a pale sludge collect up in the bowl, the answers to a hundred questions you wish had never been posed.

But my gut told me they were wrong.

My gut told me that if I couldn't find any trace of the beginning, it was because Mel's disappearance began with someone *other* than Mel, someone who clung to the shadows still. My sister's absence was a story without a beginning. A story whose origins, if they could be traced at all, were traced from a dead centre whose location we could only guess at.

There was no moment she was last seen.

She disappeared while we slept.

So I look to her things, to what was left in her closet and drawers, and in the end, from this sum of absences, I compose a picture of my sister in faded Levis, a floret of blue beads on the back pocket. In the picture I make for Mom, my sister is wearing her hippie shirt, a white blouse with sky-blue threading, a low rounded collar. I picture her warm, protected from elements, the rain and the wind, in her favourite old jeans jacket, worn threadbare at the elbows. Until Val skateboards up to our door and, looking past me and into the house, thrusts a musty heap into my hands and asks if Mel's home yet.

As I unfold the jacket, Mom's hands start to shake and she lights a cigarette from the burning stub of the last. Val flips up her board with a kick and walks into the house, but Mom stays where she is. She leans against the doorframe, pulling in so much smoke that the ember is drawn to the filter's quick. Hands trembling, she pictures you alone out there and cold.

— 3 —
Karin

Fred Irving.

A retired uniform who can't shake the habit of work. Forty years at one job will do that to a person. He retired from the force, but he's still working. Writes for the local paper. Did a piece on Mel. Still trains dogs for the department. Rottweilers, German Shepherds. The smart, mean breeds. Takes on a Lab or two, sometimes a retriever, for recovery work. Quiet man. The kind to like his dinner in front of the television. Set down on a tray. A creature of habit. A widower. Vulnerable for a man of his age.

Fred Irving made sense at that time. He made phone calls and understood what the police were talking about. Translated them for me. Kept track of things. Wrote them down. The kind of man to get things done. I needed someone around who'd get things done.

My father, the illness, the same thing. The *very* same thing.

Dad relied on us to look him in the eyes. To count out the day's pills. To make his pain manageable. To measure it in minutes, not hours. In milligram doses, not days. Dave and I made maps out of his calendar. Pathways that increased his dose of steroids. Pathways that levelled it off. Blue dots for radiation sessions and later, when that failed, red ones for chemo. You focus on details, and there's less time to think about the cancer inside of you. And when all of that failed, as it does, and the details fall away, I sat by his bed and held his hand and brushed the last of his hair from the sheets.

After two years, I'd like to say that Mel isn't dead.

I'd like to say to you, *I know.*

She's out there. Alive. I *know* it.

I know no such thing.

I read the newspaper every morning. Clip stories. The ones about the mothers who have lost their children. In crowded malls. On camping trips. During natural disasters. Unnatural ones, too. I clip the stories about mothers who *know*. *Know* their child is alive. I've got a shoebox full of stories. Of women searching for children who vanished years ago. Of women who say they *know* their children are out there. Of mothers who wait years for news. Wait forever. I read their stories and know, dead to rights, that their children are gone. When it comes to my own girl, I don't know a thing.

There are days when these newspaper mothers are the only friends I've got.

— 4 —
Lora

On the front steps, our second-door down neighbour is talking to Mr. Irving, holding him up with stories of dead husbands, her theories of the afterlife.

The phone rings, and again, it's like a switch flicks off, because the noise we amount to is shunted into silence and guarded breaths. At the door, Fred Irving and the neighbour are quiet. Limbs tense up. Mugs of coffee are held aloft, or carefully and quietly set down. Uncle Dave lifts the phone from its cradle and puts it to his ear. Holds up a finger, as if he's testing the wind. He repeats everything the caller says for our benefit. He says, "Yes, Constable Rankin, that's right, they found her things. At the subway. Islington. Yeah, we've got them already, right here. We'll see you in an hour or so." All the while, Uncle Dave watches Mom and nods, checking in. Mom clutches her knees. She looks like a hypothermia victim, wrapped up in the old blue throw.

That's when I see the look on Val's face.

While everyone is talking, Val slips out of the kitchen and heads for the stairs. I follow after her.

Upstairs, Val has let herself into Mel's room. I find her pushing aside the dirty laundry and scrabbling at the floorboards in my sister's room. Lifting a loose plank, she retrieves a metal box. A second later, she's pulled a key from under Mel's mattress.

"What's this?"

"C'mon," she says, "we need to put it all back."

I make the bed while Val restores the laundry. Satisfied, we head to my room. Only when I've put the latch in place does she relax. She camps out at the pillow end of my bed, the box next to her, and I sit by her feet.

"Why are you hiding your shit in my sister's room?"

"Relax, runt," Val says, "everything's under control."

Val opens the box.

Inside, there are a couple zine-style comic books, a diary, and a skull pipe. A tiny waxen envelope holds two purple microdots. There's something else, too. A note. Scrawled on the back of a gum wrapper.

It reads: "Stay the fuck out of my stuff. This means you."

The 'fuck' is underlined twice and the note is signed "Your sister, Mel."

I take the note. Examine the handwriting. "I never knew about the stupid box," I say.

Val pockets the wax envelope and I reach for the blue notebook. "But she would've never gone anywhere without her diary," I say.

"See there, she'll be back."

Val's words sound empty.

"Shouldn't we give this to someone? It's proof she didn't run."

"Yeah, maybe it's proof of that and maybe it's not. And then again, maybe it's proof of a whole lot of things, and maybe those things have nothing to do with Mel being gone. We need to read it before we show it to *anybody*."

That's when we hear it. The familiar creak.

— 5 —

I stand on the threshold of Mel's bedroom. The old woman from two doors down stands in front of Mel's dresser, her fingers running down the spine of Mel's comb. She reads the cards for old ladies in the co-op. Today, these hands picture things as they trace patterns on Mel's belongings. She touches the light brown hairs that have collected in the comb's plastic ribs, dips fingers into the snake-heap of bracelets pooled in an old ceramic cereal bowl. The woman sees me and still, she looks at Mel's things, touches them. Her fingers trace an outline on Mel's oval hand mirror, a gift from Nanna Stokes. She slides opens a drawer. And somehow, touching Mel's things, she knows that my sister will be found at a friend's.

"Yes," she says, "I'm sure of it. She's alive. She's crouched and scared, but breathing. I can hear that clear as day. Scratchy. At a house, I'm seeing a girl — I can only see the back of the head. I'm seeing a girl with black hair, not a friend I'd say, not someone she's close to, was close to, before, but not now."

The old woman pauses, looks disturbed. Fred Irving leans into the doorframe, notebook in hand, listening.

"Wait. Maybe? Yes, maybe it's a boy's room. Is this familiar?" she asks.

Val nods, riveted. Looks from the dresser to the old woman's hands.

"Could it be that she's with a boy? A boy she knows, but isn't so close to, one with black hair. Very black. Blood black. It's so hard to tell a girl from a boy these days," she says, "what with how they all wear their hair the same. But yes, I'm certain now, it's a young man and she's alive, that one's sister, at a house, I see inside of the walls of a dark room, I'm seeing from inside of the walls, hearing her scratchy breathing. She's with us in the walls."

"Woody," Val says, "That's Woodrow Kunzli, the freak. Exactly. I swear to God if he's hurt her, I swear, I'll make him pay."

"I don't think it's the Woodsman," I say, but already, the old woman's hands are coming for me. Pale, like the hands of someone newly dead or a hospital nurse in latex gloves. One pale finger comes at me. The air around me grows thick and the pale thing pushes at me. Before it can make contact, I push past Mr. Irving and run to the bathroom. Slam the door, slip the hook into its eye latch and turn the faucets on full.

A moment later, Val is leaning against the door, scratching after me.

"You okay?" she asks. "C'mon in there, you all right?"

"Get her out."

"But she knows things," Val says. "She can help us."

"Get her the fuck out," I scream, "get her out."

Twenty minutes later, I walk downstairs. In the kitchen, Mom's folded up the throw and stashed it on the chair back. She's wiping all of the counters down with Clorox bleach.

The smell so strong it burns my eyes.

"Don't go anywhere," she tells me without glancing up, "they're going to want to talk to you. You and Val both." She turns and looks at me hard. "You tell them everything they want to know, you hear?"

"Yes, Mom," I say. "Mom, I want her back too."

"I know you do," she says, gently, "so no holding back."

I start up the steps and then turn back.

"Mom, do you believe in happy endings?"

Mom's quiet for a while. Her eyes very far away.

"You should," she says.

"Yeah?"

"I don't think it does any harm, sweetheart."

I nod, but I'm not so sure.

— 6 —

While we wait for the officers, Val plays a game of pyramid in the living room. Uncle Dave and Garry Baxter share a smoke on the patio steps. Mom sits by the telephone, quietly talking with the man from two streets over, the one wearing the longshoreman's jacket. Mom says Mr. Irving doesn't count as a stranger. He used to be a cop, she says, and writes for the local paper. Mel used to sit for his girl, who was always with the Woodsman's younger brother. The two would lean their heads together, as if speaking a language only each other knew. One that flew between their minds with that slim contact.

Mom talks quietly, slowly, doling out each of her words as if they are difficult to let go of, and Mr. Irving, sometimes he jots a word or two down in a little black notebook, but for the most part, he rests one hand on Mom's hand, the two of them seated across from one another at the table, and looks at Mom in a searching way. His eyes are very dark, so dark that it looks like they are all pupil, the kind of eyes that are without a centre.

While they're talking, Fred looks for Mel. He looks for her in my mom's face and in the story of Mel's hospital admission. He even looks for her in the photos on the fridge. And then I realize that, half-hidden by the photo of Mel and me, is an old welfare stub. He stands up and walks over to the fridge, thumbs the old cheque stub, its edge visible under a photo. The stub is from the summer I was twelve and Mel thirteen and Mom got fired, this time from Towers. His eyes return to the photo, and I come and stand next to him, look at the picture too.

At first, all I see is Mel and me. The two of us are standing in the living room, dressed up for Halloween. Mel's a pretty black cat and me, I'm in my big fat peach suit, the one Mom made out of hangers and an old bedsheet and that I loved, unreasonably, for no other reason than it suited me perfectly, absurdly, and if I could have, I would have worn it every day. I felt as small and safe as a secret inside of that big peach-coloured sphere, my head a grinning stem. Then I see what's behind us in the photo, the white threads that have been laid bare, the pulled stuffing, the place where the Naugahyde sofa is worn bare, a spot Mom covers with the throw when she thinks of it, and in front of the sofa, a stain on the carpet I'd never noticed. I look up at the real carpet. See what's left of the stain. Grape juice scrubbed down to a patch of dull grey. The photo is held in place with an animal magnet. A pink caterpillar. Old smashed pipe cleaners for legs, glued to a dusty string of pom-poms. A little rectangular magnet on the under-side of its belly.

I want to tell Mr. Irving that the only reason we've kept the stupid caterpillar is because Mel made it when she was a little kid, she made it for Mom, who keeps *every*thing. Only if I tried to explain the bug, I wouldn't know where to stop. Because here we are, where everything in the world our family has amounted to is col-lected up in one place, and all of it looks like cheap seconds at a garage sale. No, not even. More like the free box you put out at the end of the sale, next to the garbage bins, when the sun's gone down and you realize that you can't unload what you've got on anyone at any price.

The feeling doesn't last.

Soon, any shame I might've felt is gone, has retreated back to a tiny nucleus, very dense and small, like a grain of rice in a football stadium. It's strange. I guess most kids in my place would hate Fred Irving. Or better, hate Trudy Semple, who fits into *every*thing and is adored by *every*-one, students and teachers alike. My life would be simpler if I hated Trudy Semple since she's the kind of girl who could never disappear, since someone is *always* looking at her, *always*. It'd be simpler, too, if I hated the uniformed strangers who walk into our house, because of the way they look at us as evidence, too unwieldy for plastic bags, and so, the worst kind of possible proof. I see it in their eyes. How hard *they* find it to talk to *us*. It's as if *we* should feel sorry for *them*. But no, when Mr. Irving looks at the welfare stub, and a moment later looks away, as if he's embarrassed for us, and so, is pretending not to have seen, and when the uniform flinches a second after he asks if Mel would have a reason to run away from home, and when our second-door down neighbour wipes the dust from Mel's chest of drawers with her sweater's sleeve, and glances up at me, her eyes twin apologies, I look at us through their eyes and for a second, a split second, I get it. I see them seeing us and I see, too, why it is we can just disappear.

— 7 —

For days it goes on and nothing looks right. The sun is paler than usual, bleached out, and the whole world looks stage-lit. I'm not being dramatic. Kids run away all the time and it doesn't change anything. Only when Mel disappears, something does change. More than in my head. Something *out there*. When I look out the door, I can see that the air is heavier and I know that anything could happen to any one of us.

Could have happened.

To Mel.

And then comes the moment when I can't *not* know the worst is coming.

A few hours before the uniforms arrive, the world breaks into before and after pictures in my head, and everything, *everything* changes. Mom and Mr. Baxter walk through the front door, Mel's stuff in hand, and I don't think anybody else hears it, but there's this little popping sound. I look around me but I'm pretty sure the noise must've come from inside of my head.

Mom sets down Mel's things on the coffee table, and next thing you know, Uncle Dave is catching at Mom as she falls, and her body is crumpling up in a way I didn't know a body could.

Uncle Dave pulls her back up, holds her so she's facing him. He looks into her eyes as if the steadiness of his gaze alone can hold her up.

"It's her birthday," Mom says, muttering at the floor. I barely hear her. "I haven't gotten anything," Mom says. "I was going to stop at the mall yesterday, but then, and now...."

Mel's sixteenth birthday.

We'd forgotten.

I pick up Mel's glasses. Cut my finger on the broken edge.

− 8 −

Wherever Mel is, whatever has happened to her, it's been done without her to bear witness.

I once asked Mel what it was like when she took her glasses off and she described to me a world in which everything became soft, edges bristling into a hint of innumerable fine threads. People drifted past her calmly, like low-lying clouds. When she took off her glasses, she tended to remain still, drawing back from anyone that approached. It was as if contact would ruin the illusion. When she described her world, it sounded a little bit like being in heaven.

After she disappeared, I thought about the tattoo.

The tiny tattoo on the small of her back, which, if her body was ever found, would upset Mom terribly. A tattoo and beneath it, her initials, M.A.S.

My initials, too.

When the police asked me if there are any

identifying marks, I couldn't say. I couldn't say without Mom finding out about Mel's tattoo and by implication, my own. I could only hope Mel was okay, that Mom never need find out.

They let me keep a pair of her glasses.

I kept her second-best glasses and put them on sometimes.

We never got the best pair back.

When I put on Melissa's old glasses, ones she's outgrown, I can feel the younger Mel looking out at the world through me, from the time we were closest.

Camp Totoredaka. August 1981.

I put on her old glasses, and it's as if her eyes, her vision, happens outside of her a little, where her sight meets the thick glass inside the black frames. Her younger self is gathered there. When I put on Melissa's old glasses, the world becomes soft and indistinct.

And then my eyes begin to compensate, focus in on a shifting middle ground.

My eyes exist in this focus, this absolute clarity, where I can see everything perfectly, but what I see is out of reach. Melissa's eyesight rims this place. Her eyes are seeing everything near to me when I am focused on everything remote. When I look to what is closest, Melissa flags my vision, so the edges come undone, are soft and unsettled.

Wherever Melissa turns her eyes, everything dissolves into the nebulous nothing she always suspected it was.

I put on her glasses so I can see with her eyes.

Her eyes make everything hard and sharp about this world draw back. The way I imagine it is inside of her body, inside of the nasal passage, the lungs, where everything is coated with a fine layer of cilia. Inside of this passage, nothing moves of its own volition but, as she draws each breath, is gently moved by countless fine hairs.

Camp Totoredaka for two weeks at the end of summer. We are the closest. Ever. Twelve years old, and assigned to the same tribe at day camp. We sit together on the bus, both ways. It's the very last summer Mel wears these glasses, with the thick black frames.

There are beautiful places, fields and forests. Our tribe leaves these behind, on our hike, and discovers desolate fields, pale cracked dirt. What industry leaves behind. First generation scrub. We come upon a wash, covered over with algae. A foundation has been dug in and then abandoned. It has captured a summer's worth of rain. On the side of the bowl, there is a derelict refrigerator. Lying on its back. Three or four of us, high on Kool-Aid and chocolate, approach.

Mel and I stand on either side. It takes both of us to pull the door open. Gravity, I guess. It has only recently been abandoned. Contents crawling with maggots.

Mel coughs, her eyes watering. She pulls off the glasses to try and stop the smell.

Wednesdays. For an extra twelve dollars, day camp extends overnight.

That's twenty-four dollars for Mel and me. Sometimes Mom thinks it's worth it. More Kool-Aid. Hot dogs for dinner. S'mores for dessert. A campfire. Campfire songs.

Seven or eight strung out twelve-year-olds in each of a dozen old army tents. You have to bring your own sleeping bag. And then, there is what happens after the ghost stories, when we're alone in our tents.

"You lie here, in the middle," Mel instructs.

"Everybody else go around.

"No, everyone has to kneel or it won't work.

"No, not you, Lora. Just lay there.

"Now, close your eyes and concentrate.

"It won't work if you don't close your eyes.

"You *have* to close them.

"Now, say it now."

Sometimes the dead are light, so light, six children can lift the tiny body with the tips of their fingers. Chanting together, *you are light as a feather, light as a feather, light as a feather*. But without the invocation, the dead are immeasurably heavy, so heavy, you cannot lift them at all.

— 9 —

It was at summer camp, the August we were twelve, that me and Mel began to switch. People didn't notice the height. They focused in on the glasses to tell us apart. And so, we could dip into one another's lives and, for a little while, we'd become unsure of where one of us ended and the other began. We switched so easily, so completely, who was who was who would blur. And all it took, the signal, was the Coke-bottle glasses. Our eyes became the same eyes.

As ourselves, she with her glasses and me without, we saw the world with the same cold clarity. As each other, me with her glasses and she without, we found an indistinct landscape in which colourful shapes moved in and out of our range of vision. She lived completely inside of this cloudy place, and I looked in from the outside. My eyes, adjusting to the strong lens, carved out a circle of sanity in the midst of that place, one which smudged into obscurity at the edges. There was only ever that clear middle ground, always a little out of reach, to remind me of where she might have ended and where I might have begun.

When we switched, her life went on, smoothly, without her in it.

We fit snugly into the gaps in each other's experiences. This changed us both. By the time she was gone, I don't think either of us was capable of taking our lives very personally anymore.

After she was gone, I began to think about the different ways she might have gone.

I didn't mean to. But it kept happening.

All that empty space she left behind her, it was too much. It started filling up with stories, the way the wash we'd stumbled on as children collected up all of the summer's inadvertent rain.

Sometimes, with Mel's glasses on, the world gets lost. And then Mom looks up at me from the middle ground, remote in its clarity, and her eyes start to water.

Until she peers past the thick glass and into my eyes, I can tell, for an instant, she takes me for Mel. Mom doesn't say anything and I'm grateful. Mom knows how much I miss her.

I don't know why Mom doesn't cry.

I don't know where she thinks Mel is.

I cry.

I cry in the bathroom with the water running. It's as if I need permission and running water gives me that.

Mom doesn't cry.

She sees me in Mel's old glasses and for an instant, I think she might, but instead, she puts her hands on my shoulders and asks me, please, to finish making the lists.

We all heard the click and turned to see Nanna opening the storm door. Mom took a deep breath and walked forward, nodding. She kissed Nanna on her cheek.

"I've known you since you were fourteen years old," Nanna told her. "I know you, girl, like the back of my very hand. Since you were fourteen years old and loved my boy."

Mom nodded.

It was as close as I've seen Mom come to admitting she loved Dad.

"We could use help," Mom told her. "There's certain kinds of help you can give."

She meant money. We all knew that.

"Whatever it is you need," Nanna said, patting Mom's hand, "you'll have it."

Nanna breezed down the hall, stopping to give me a kiss, her shawl billowing. In her wake I could smell the Eaton's perfume counter at Christmas, pretty salesgirls and silk scarves. I rubbed the fuchsia-pink imprint from my cheek as Nanna headed for the centre of things: the diminished group seated around the telephone at the kitchen table.

I hadn't seen my grandmother since the last Thanksgiving. Mom had been edgier than usual. As soon as the last bite was down our gullets, and before Nanna had cleared the dinner dishes, Mom had our coats in hand.

Mel had other ideas. She dawdled. Slowly trawled a spoon through the ice cream and ate her apple pie one tiny bite at a time. Inside my parka, I sweated and watched Mel eat. Or rather, I watched her play at eating. Mom took off her jacket and sighed, folding it in her lap.

"The traffic's bad, I bet," Mom said to no one in particular.

"She thinks he's going to show up," I told her, turtling out of my parka.

"What?"

"She thinks if she draws it out long enough," I said, "that Dad will show up."

"Why don't you tell these girls he's not coming?"

Our eyes were on our grandmother, instantly.

"Oh, you want me to tell them about your son?" Mom asked. It sounded like a threat.

Mel stared into her melted ice cream, as if she could read the future there. When Mel was upset, she looked closer to twelve than fifteen.

"Your father," Nanna Stokes said, her eyes not once leaving our mother, "is not on his way to this house." There was a certainty in her voice that was disconcerting.

"Your father's not dead," Mom said, "but I promise you one thing, you won't be running into your father on the street, not anytime soon."

That was it. End of subject. Miserable, Mel pushed back her bowl and picked up her coat. Still, it wasn't until I saw Nanna Stokes breeze into our home, sails billowing, that I realized Dad was truly off the map. The worst had come to pass, Mel was gone, and there was no sign of him.

I trailed into the kitchen after Nanna.

"Maybe they're together," I said.

"Who?" Nanna asked. She was focused on the list Officer Groves had given us the first night. The one that outlined the steps we should take. They had a list for that. Mimeographed and waiting in a drawer.

"Mel and Dad."

Nanna Stokes set the paper down on the table and looked up, past me, to Mom.

"I'll talk to her," Mom said. "When the moment's right."

Nanna raised an eyebrow. But the subject was dropped. Neither had so much as looked my way. Nanna Stokes shook her head, picked up the phone and dialled.

"Cathy, it's Celia. Put Garry on the phone, would you?"

"Yes, I'm here, at Karin's house. I wonder, are you still in, ahm, how shall I put it? touch, are you still in *touch*, with that redhead of yours?" Nanna untied the silk scarf from her neck.

"It's her daughter I want to talk with, she had a daughter in the, not the P.I. business, but, no, that's right, she spent her summers at a credit agency, that's right. A skip tracer." With that, Claire Laba, a Ph.D. candidate in forensic anthropology, daughter of a real redhead, was ushered into our lives.

— 11 —

I gave Mom my shoebox of scraps, lists written on the inside of cigarette packs, receipts, *Hello Kitty* stationery, napkins and three-ring binder paper. Some of the lists were dotted with scratch-and-sniff stickers. Mom scratched one that claimed to be strawberry, but it was so old that all the sticker gave off was a faint brown stink. She scrunched up her nose, lifted half a dozen scraps of paper in her hand and let them fall back into the box. Handed it to me.

"Sweetie," she said, "I want you to go wash your face," and after I did, she sat me down at the kitchen table and gave me a glass of milk, like I was a kid, and after I'd drunk it, she said, "You know you're my beautiful girl."

I nodded.

She touched my face.

"I want you to make me a list of the lists you've made. That way," she said, "the Laba woman can ask you for what she needs. Tonight.

Can you do that for me?"

I nodded and Mom told me what a good job Val and I were doing. What good helpers we were. She may have been treating me like an eight-year-old, but I was grateful. As Val watched television, I sat down with my shoebox and made a list of the lists I'd made. Until that moment, I hadn't realized how badly I wanted something to come after. For there to be one thing and then some other thing after that. The big list, the list of all the others, let me know that.

Val flicked through the channels at lightning speed and a barrage of lights and colours flickered over her face. She stopped on channel ten. The local cable station.

A chorus of grade twos played the theme song from M*A*S*H on wooden recorders. The sound was wistful, defeated. A teacher stood before the kids, waving her arms in big circles and the wet marks under her arms looked like the protective colouring of some new butterfly. Val mouthed the lyrics to the song and in my head, the last few days begin to be reordered. Whatever it was that'd been lodged in my throat was gone. The sad lump had been swallowed down into the pit of me and I knew I'd wake up, and that Val would too, and we'd make ourselves a bite to eat, and one step at a time, we'd do whatever we had to do to find Mel. That's when it occurred to me. If we wanted to get to the truth, if we wanted to really find my sister, we'd need help.

"Val," I said, "remember the time you broke into Howlett's van?"

"Oh man," Val shook her head. "That was an accident."

"Yeah, whatever, look, there's something I need from the van."

"The pistol?"

"I need people to take me seriously," I quietly told her.

"You know it's only a starter pistol."

I looked at her, unhappily, and waited.

"I guess it's better than nothing," she said and gazed at the ceiling. "Yeah, yeah, I'll get it." Val exhaled into her bangs.

I watched the uniforms select Mel's things, choose what to preserve in evidence bags. I waited for them to go through her bedroom, but it didn't happen. Val had been worried for nothing. The officers had a much simpler plan: to ask. They collected our words in lieu of things. They asked if Mom had found anything, a note, a diary entry, and when she shook her head, they asked if she'd look again, "give it a *good* look," they told her.

I waited for the uniforms to slide a hand under Mel's mattress, search through her desk and dresser drawers. Instead, they took down an account from Mr. Baxter, of where and how her things had been found at the subway, while Mom checked Mel's room for some secret sign my sister had known she was leaving us. Val and I stood in the doorway and watched. Mom's back was shaking as she felt her way under the mattress. And then she stopped. Turned her back to the bed and sat down on the floor. She ran her hands over her face and muttered, "fuck it, fuck it."

I'd never heard my mother swear like that before. *Never.*

I came and sat by her side, putting my arm around her shoulders.

"I can do this, Mom," I said. "It's okay."

Mom nodded, but didn't move.

Fred came and stood in the doorway, awkwardly shifting his weight from one foot to the other. At another time, it would have struck me as hilarious, the little dance he did. I would have whispered cracks to Val about pubic lice.

"What do they want with her diary, anyways," Val wanted to know. "I mean, *if* she has one."

I rolled my eyes.

"The answers," Mom said, "they want all of the answers, all neatly lined up in a row, and laid out for them just like that."

"If you find anything," Fred said, "keep it to yourself."

I looked up at him. We all did.

Val raised an eyebrow, gave me an *I told you so* look.

Fred talked slowly, watching Mom's face all the while. "If your daughter is anything like every other teenage girl I've ever worked, and if it's evidence of her miserable home life they're looking for, they'll find it. Until we know more, until we see some real action on their part, don't hand them an excuse to stop looking for the girl. Look, give it to me, I'll read it over myself, to see what there is to it, and we'll pass on anything significant, but let's not make it easy for them to dismiss this."

"That's *if* she has a diary," Val repeated.

I gave Val a look.

I hadn't seen Mel's box since we'd first found it and realized that Val could've hidden it anywhere in the last two days, inside of the house or out. I had the feeling I wouldn't see it again either. Not until Val was good and ready to *let* me see it. I looked at Mr. Irving and then at Val. It struck me, weirdly, that the two weren't so different.

I was out of my league with Fred *and* Val and I knew it. They were both a hundred thousand times tougher than I'd ever be.

— 13 —

The police wanted our stories. They wanted our stories, and they wanted them laid out from A to Z. But Claire was different. In the movies, the police come in full force and so do the others, the ones who wear gloves.

Not in real life.

In real life, if any of them don gloves, it's only to avoid getting their hands dirty while looking through a stranger's things for obvious answers, like a diary entry about how much home life sucks and how great it'd be to run away, or a suicide pact written in blood.

The uniforms went through Mel's knapsack, but they ignored the telling clues. The ones that told you who Mel was. They never went into her room, and so never saw the pictures of me and Val, Ronnie and the Woodsman, of Jules, tacked up in a collage on her wall, heads scissored from old photos and pasted onto a kaleidoscope of cartoon bodies. They didn't witness the way that her favourite stuffed animals waited for her, lined up on the bed in a motley chorus, the big old bear wearing an AC/DC concert shirt that Mel had kept clean, unworn, like a museum piece.

Claire was different.

Claire looked at everything, thoughtfully, a little aimlessly even.

I walked into my sister's room to find Claire searching in ways the police hadn't. She was holding Buster, my sister's favourite, up to her face. I knew the bear smelled of dull corkboard and my sister's hair, shampooed nightly, so there was a hint of something tart and sweet on her pillow, like freshly sliced apples. Here was some-one who wasn't scared of Mel, wasn't scared of what it meant that she was gone, or of how much we missed her. I trusted Claire when I saw her breathe in my sister's smell.

"What are you doing?" I asked.

She tucked a strand of rich auburn hair behind her ear, held out her hand and said to me, "Oh, hello, I'm Claire."

There was something I needed to understand. I'd watched the policeman go through my sister's things. They'd shoved aside her math binder, inked with lyrics, while making a label for the bag that held my sister's hairbrush. I remember, the officer had looked at me apologetically as what remained of Mel's soft brown hair, glinting with the last of the day's light, was placed in the kind of plastic bag goldfish come home from the pet store in. It was the only evidence they'd bagged that day. That and the broken glasses.

"So how exactly are they supposed to find my sister with a hairbrush and glasses put into plastic baggies?" I asked her.

"Science, you mean?"

I nodded, though I wasn't sure what I'd meant.

"Do you know where the word *science* comes from?" she asked. "It comes from the Latin word *scire*," she said, "*to know*. And you want *to know*, right?"

I nodded again.

"Science isn't going to give you the answers you want," she said. "Science is one kind of knowing, a divisive, a *cut off* kind of knowing. In Latin, *scire* means to know, and to know is to separate things out. It's related to *scindere*, *to cut*. So, perhaps a forensic scientist could tell you some physical facts based on what your sister left behind and even tell you who has been in a room, but they can't tell you what she's doing now. They can't tell you where she is. And I'll tell you one other fundamental fact science can't know. Science can't know *who* she is.

"Science comes from *scire*, a word that

shares its roots with scissors and shit. If I'd kept up on my Latin," she said, placing the bear on the pillow, "I'd have gone into the Humanities." And then she looked at me, full on, and smiled. Claire had a warm smile. The kind of smile that radiates, like warm sunshine. The smile left her, but not the kindness, as she said, "Science and shit share the same root. Remember that. I don't want anything that might be coming to be any harder on you than it has to be."

"Are you like some kind of cop?"

"No," she laughed, "I'm not with the police." Claire took off her glasses and rubbed the lens on her shirt. "Garry Baxter was your father's friend, right? They grew up together."

This I knew. I nodded.

"Well, for a long time, he was my mother's friend too...." She let the thought trail off. "I have certain skills that may assist you now, and Celia, your grandmother, has hired me to use those skills on your behalf, to work in *your* interests, not the public's, but yours and Mel's. That means I'm here to look out for you and your sister. Understand?"

That I understood. Perfectly.

While the officers labelled Mel's brush, I'd looked at the scuffs on Mel's boot, the pattern of tar scuffed onto the left sole, so like a finger-print, and at the thick-lensed glasses Mel wore on the day she disappeared, cracked now, and without which she was unable to read so much as the expression on someone's face. If they'd wanted to know a thing about my sister, it was this they should have examined: the thickness of Mel's broken lens and the swirling black tar on the sole of her boot.

Without her glasses, my sister was sightless. Had she turned, dropping her glasses? Had she tried to face someone she could no longer see?

One thing became clear, though, and it made my blood run cold. As the two officers were leaving, Constable Rankin, who'd taken Mr. Baxter's statement, told Officer Singh where the janitor had found Mel's things. As he told his partner about the dumpster, I saw a shadow pass across Singh's eyes.

Val must've seen it too. Sensed it.

The void that was opening up and swallowing more and more of Mel.

"There've been others," I heard Val say.

Fred Irving's head whipped around to look at Val.

It was the first time I'd heard Val acknowledge that something had happened to Mel. And it came out in a whisper. So quiet I was sure the police hadn't heard her.

"There've been others," Mr. Baxter repeated, loudly. Impossible to ignore.

Officer Singh turned to Baxter.

"How many?" Mr. Baxter demanded.

"Unofficially?"

Mr. Baxter shrugged. For the first time, I was glad Mr. Baxter was nobody's fool.

"It's not the first time," Singh admitted, "a missing girl's things have been found next to a dumpster. Not the first time a missing girl's things have been recovered at Islington or Kipling or thereabouts."

"There's been five or six. Probably runaways," Rankin added. "Look, that's all there is to it. I don't know that there's a link."

When the officer referred to Mel as *missing*, and not as a runaway, the cold that had first taken up residence in me the day Mel disappeared began to collect up in my bones once again. I was shivering uncontrollably.

— 15 —

Claire was examining the collage Mel had made, the one of me and Jules, Val and Ronnie, and the Woodsman. Several versions of our heads, with a range of expressions, had been pasted onto the bodies of Bugs Bunny and Wile E. Coyote, Elmer Fudd and Tweety and the like. Now and again, Mel had returned to the collage, pencilling in horns and mustaches. Thought bubbles formed a perennial series of afterthoughts.

I looked more closely.

"The police say there've been others," I told Claire, and noticed that Mel had added a line drawing of a nuclear explosion. A mushroom cloud bloomed across the horizon, spreading its poison over all of our heads. The cloud's stem emanated from somewhere behind us. Beside the poisonous blossom, my sister, the budding eco-terrorist, had scribbled in a thought bubble: "Unlike fossil fuels, hate burns clean."

Val came and stood next to me, and I could

smell stale smoke. Claire didn't look up. She examined the collage very closely. It was as if she hadn't heard me.

"That's my fave," Val said and pointed at a portrait Mel had done of Val's head pasted onto a ridiculously tiny body that swirled round and round, a hurricane with two tiny feet akimbo, a tiny skateboard flying up out of the dust. "You've met the runt," Val said, pointing at a picture of me, "and that's Ronnie, preggers, and that," she said, pointing to ground zero, "that's Mel's boyfriend or whatever, that's Jules."

Claire's eyebrows furrowed as she looked at Val. "And where's he now?"

I don't think his absence had occurred to me.

Val looked at Claire and shrugged.

— 16 —
Celia

Fred Irving. Retired from the force. Writes for the local paper now. A hobby of sorts. I see his name next to the occasional op-ed. You know the sort, panic pieces, the usual thin arguments for harsher sentences. My interest in such writing is, let's say, anthropological.

At the time my granddaughter went missing, Irving was active, writing a mini-crime beat, four to five column inches each week in which he gave a rundown of local criminal activity, well, what they considered criminal in the west end of Mississauga at that time, which wasn't an "end" in practice as so much as theory, one undergoing an awkward translation from farmland to suburb and which was still, in places like the McCauley Green, a muttish hybrid, strip malls giving out onto cornfields and lawless semi-detacheds rising each morning out of patches of freshly flattened muck. Incidents such as that awful shooting of Barbara Turnbull were the exception, not the rule. So, when I say crime beat, what I mean is that if the local Tim Hortons was held up for a hundred dollars by a twelve year old with a BB gun, well, that'd be half of Irving's column inches for the week, though he did the odd feature from time to time, *Local Girl Wins Spelling Bee,* and the like. I suppose the piece he wrote on Melissa was his biggest, before or since, which isn't to say the suburbs are some kind of a respite from the urban degeneration faced elsewhere. There's something in the faces of these girls that tells me otherwise. I saw it in the older girl, and I see it in the younger one too sometimes. Not always, but at times. The same hooded look I see in the eyes of the girl behind the counter of the coffee shop, a half smoked cigarette tucked behind her ear, and in the heavy-lidded eyes of the girls I see loitering in their lumberjackets and cut-offs around the mall food court, emptying sugar packets onto the faux-wood tables and, in the spill of white crystals, spelling out the initials of god-knows-who. There is a wariness to those girls, a tenacity, and what that tells me is there are conditions here which foster both of these qualities.

So, yes, *Local Girl Goes Missing.*

I remember the piece. I remember him talking to my daughter-in-law before the piece ran.

It was important to him that it run *above the fold*. Above the fold, he made a big push for it. If the picture wasn't right, if the story didn't strike the right nerve with his editor, or worse, there was no nerve struck at all, he wouldn't be able to get the story *above the fold*.

Fred wanted to go with a different photo than the one that ran, ultimately. He favoured one that wasn't recent, that was Karin's objection, though I suppose the picture he preferred gave my granddaughter something of the look that newspaper editors and the like believe that missing girls have, or should have, if the image is to sell copy: in this case, the preternatural child. I remember it *was* a lovely photograph, there was something haunting about it, specifically around the eyes. Something to do with the play of light and shadow I never quite put my finger on. A September school photo, from the year before. Something of the fourteen-year-old to her in that picture, a bit of the child she was clinging to the edges of her mouth, her eyes, and a sensuality too, a hint, in the fullness of her mouth, but it was her, no mistaking it, you could recognize her easily which might have set my daughter-in-law at ease. But it didn't. It didn't set her at ease.

Karin said she couldn't take the chance someone would see her daughter and think, no, that can't be the girl, the missing one's younger than her and she insisted Fred go with the most recent, a Polaroid taken after a party, that would be my guess, and in which, it is true, the girl looks a little less than innocent. Perhaps it is the smudged kohl under her eyes that makes her look world-weary at fifteen, or perhaps it's the attitude she bore whoever took the photograph. Regardless, the Polaroid was only a few months old, the most recent picture we had and, for all of its flaws, resembled my granddaughter more than any other. Precisely because of its flaws.

A couple of years later, a technician, one who volunteered with a non-profit agency for missing children, manufactured a new picture of my granddaughter, in which our girl was progressed to eighteen, and in the progression, I am sure I see a preference, again, for the play of light and dark in that school photo. It's in how they've let her irises fall into shadow. Something you'd see in a Caravaggio. The eyes in the progression put me in mind of Judith in Caravaggio's painting of Holofernes's beheading, though I must say I prefer the brutal sheets of Gentileschi's Judith to the soft arms and squeamish brow of the Caravaggio.

In the end, of course, as Fred foretold, his storyline appeared down in the bottom right corner of the front page, about as far *below* the fold as it could be. After an inch of text was the line: *continued on A9*, which might not be so distressing in a large paper, but the A was a bit of a pretense, as there was only ever a B section in the Saturday edition, and this was Wednesday, and besides, the entirety of that issue was perhaps ten pages. So it was there, on the next to last page, sandwiched between one story about land development and another about the local varsity football team that a murky, nearly illegible version of the Polaroid appeared. In the reproduction, my granddaughter's features appear hollowed out. All the colours I've often remarked on in her beautiful eyes reduced to a smattering of black ink.

Fred's story was what you'd expect, a bit wordy for my taste, dusky adjectives casting a black veil over everything, the girl's friends included, but at the time and even now when I look at it, I can see why Karin believed it would be the start of things, that there couldn't help but be a *spate of attention* thanks to the story. It was the *spate* she was counting on. That's how we all referred to it, *the coming spate*. Of course, very few people read the local paper, which had a circulation of 5,000 at best, and a good number less would have turned to the second to last page to see the badly reproduced picture of my granddaughter and fewer still would have taken the time to guess at Melissa's features, to rough them in, so to speak, to somehow tally a girl's face from vacant spots alternating with splotches of black ink. So in some ways, the original story was on par with having no picture run at all and it was *the coming spate* which was to redress all of this.

Well, it's been three years and no spate.

So if people are familiar, at all, with the Polaroid of my granddaughter, it's through the missing posters. It's the locals who see those, ones who switch buses at the mall, or who transfer at Islington or Kipling.

On the off chance, once each month, I drive to the bus terminal downtown, at Bay and Dundas. Every fourth Sunday I drive down, now, and see how the posters I put up on my last trip have weathered, if they have, and whether they've been encroached upon by the faces of other runaways. It's a sad little anniversary I keep on my own. Do you know, the first place I go in any new city is the bus terminal? On those rare occasions I find myself in another city, I settle into my hotel room, push aside the Gideon's Bible and thumb the Yellow Pages looking for the local bus station. Next, I find a university library, one of the few places you can pay to use a photocopier. But also, I suppose, such libraries have always been a place of comfort to me, ever since, as a girl, I struggled to educate myself, not an easy task at that time. So, yes, to see all these young faces engaged in the selfsame struggle, it gives me strength.

I suppose, I hope to see – if not my granddaughter — something of her in a young girl's eyes. Sometimes, I allow myself to watch one girl in particular, from behind, and if the light glints off of her soft brown hair, I imagine for a small space that it *is* Melissa. Somehow, among the stacks, where the smell of old paper is stronger than any human scent, it's possible to believe the lies we tell. I've always found it easiest to lie to myself in a library, surrounded by a thousand improbable alternatives to what otherwise must be known, rationally, to be the case.

The fact is, her belongings, her identification, the shoes she wore the day she left, were all found dumped, like the belongings of another half-dozen so-called runaways. In a period of eighteen months, six girls vanish from the face of this earth, and their belongings are recovered at either Islington or Kipling or points between, and still, they are referred to as runaways? This when her bank account, with a balance of one hundred dollars, has not been touched, not to this day. No sixteen-year-old girl can disappear, let alone *six*. I don't care what the line is, officially speaking, teenage girls are incapable of that kind of thoroughness, they lack the discipline.

No, it's plain to see.

She's been gone these last three years without the least trace. In itself, that tells the story, leading us to the one basic, irreducible fact at the heart of all the other facts: the girl is *gone*, and after three years, what else can it mean to say that a girl is *gone*.

— 17 —
Lora

The day that my world stops looking like something a deranged high-school student might smear on bristol board in art class and begins to make something like regular sense again is September 13th, 1984, the day after Fred Irving's article comes out in the *McCauley Observer*. I hadn't yet read it. Mel had been gone for a week and Mom, she decided it was time for me to go back to school.

She trailed me to the door and kissed me on the forehead like I was a little kid.

"Mom," I said, and pulled myself from her arms. But her eyes were spun out of glass. "Sorry," I whispered, and pushed my forehead up against her mouth, squeezing her arm.

"What about Val?" I asked, "Doesn't she have to go to school?"

"She was up half the night with me. Your Uncle Dave will take her, when she gets up. On her own."

I nodded.

"Okay, see ya," I said, and waited for her to nod or say goodbye. To let me go.

"Funny Val's mother hasn't called." Mom's hand on my shoulder.

"I'm gonna miss the bus," I said.

Finally, I shrugged her hand off and turned away. Behind me, the click of the door.

Mom shut the door and the door shut on Mom. The door shut up the hole in our house front and it shut in the wet stench of grief. It was the first time in days I'd stood outside of our miserable walls, the first time I'd gotten away from the sad lot of us, and I swear, I almost cried out, it was such a relief to discover that in spite of everything gone wrong, the world was alive with rain-soaked sidewalks and the mossy smell of worms.

— 18 —

When I stepped onto the school bus, the relief evaporated. I knew I'd made a big mistake not waking Val. No, not big: *huge*. I walked up the aisle and a wave of silence descended. The whispering began in my wake. I grabbed an empty seat two rows from the back and, as the whispering built, focused on the back of the seat ahead of me, wriggled a finger into a tiny rip in the burgundy pleather, worrying it bigger so I could pick at the stuffing.

Two seats ahead of me, one of the boys had the paper open and was reading the article about my sister. He'd whisper with his friend and every so often, one or the other glanced back. I hadn't read it, though Fred had dropped five copies off the night before. I couldn't read it. I'd look at the type and my brain would turn to mud.

Two stops later, Tricia, a girl from the *Christian Fellowship Club* got on. Seeing me, she put on her very best *After-School Special* face and headed straight to the back for me. This wasn't part of her routine. She's the kind of girl who has palpitations if a wheel well separates her from the driver. On this day, she settled her butt into the seat next to me. All around me were pretty girls with soft cotton collars and precious pumps, smelling of perfumes with names like *Love's Baby Soft*.

The girl next to me sat primly on the seat and told me God was looking out for my sister. I could tell she wanted a cameo in the made-for-TV movie version of Mel's life, the one that would showcase her to the world as the kind-hearted girl who gave a shit close to the very end. When the niner in the seat ahead of me turned around to look, I recognized her. Carly Wasdell. One of the little kids Mel and me had gone to grade school with. The one whose mouth Mel had filled with tiny rocks.

"How awful it must be," she whispered, "how *perfectly* awful."

"And that ex of hers," Tricia added, "totally creepy."

"He's in my geography class." Carly's voice is a rushed whisper.

"Oh my God," said Tricia, "what's he like?"

"Jules dropped out," I say.

"No, Woodrow," she corrected. "Woodrow is in my geography class. He hasn't dropped out."

"I would drop out if I were him," said Tricia. "I mean, they'll probably put him in jail."

I tried to follow what they were saying, but everywhere I turned, there were soft-haired girls with heavily Vaselined lips who, if they weren't picturing things before I got on the bus, started to as soon as I did.

Carly Wasdell was the worst. That edge to her voice, as if she got a sweet Benzedrine rush when something truly terrible happened to someone else. Someone she *practically* knew. I could see her picturing what might have happened to Mel, reviewing the storylines of a thousand crap television shows in search of images of Mel as the runaway, the raped girl, the missing, the dead.

I stared at the rubber runner on the aisle floor. The thin black ribs that collect and hold the slimy rainwater from our boots. As Carly pattered on, it was all I could do to stop myself from slapping the pictures out of her head. Finally, I pushed past them and made my way to the empty seat behind the bus driver.

"Jesus Christ," I heard Carly mutter, "what the hell's her problem."

At Unity Gate, the Woodsman got on the school bus and sat next to me.

On the bus, the Woodsman is quiet, like me. His sister, a short-haired punk with a sweet smile and lips like bruised fruit, walked past us and took the seat behind. The Woodsman nodded at me and pulled a sheath of papers from his knapsack, swollen and crumpled. Must've had his homework with him in the bath, I thought. I pressed my head against the cool glass, and let the vibrations travel up from the wheel and jackhammer my skull. But my eyes kept drifting to the pages in his lap. The handwritten lists. Top ten and top fifty. Charts of band rankings going back almost as long as I'd known him. I thought he'd stopped making those lists up in grade seven.

"You look cold," he said.

"Sorry," I said, "I was looking at, I don't know. Sorry."

"I could raise the temperature a few degrees."

Anybody else, and I'd have known it was a trick. But the Woodsman had something soft and magical inside of him. Maybe it's that he's basically a gentle kid, one who's seen the worst of people, and still chooses to be gentle, only it isn't *for* you or because of anything that might've happened to your sister. It's his way. That makes you trust it. Trust him. I've sometimes thought gravity would suspend itself if he decided not to believe in it.

"Yeah," I said, "maybe I'm a little cold. I'm always cold."

The Woodsman focused on the thermometer hanging over the bus driver's seat. "I could bring that up to seventy degrees."

I nodded and he closed his eyes, focusing. The whispering grew quiet and fell away.

A minute passed, and as I watched, the thermometer did move and the goose pimples on my arms laid back down to sleep inside of my skin.

"Thanks."

"No prob," he shrugged. "I'm getting my car back today from shop. Want a ride home?"

"Sure," I said. "I'll meet you in the lot."

He went back to his swollen stack of papers.

"Did your band make it in the top ten again?"

He nodded.

"The Polar Bears?"

He nodded again. "I've got geography first thing. It's such crap," he said. "History, too."

I nodded.

"They sure lie a lot at this school."

I nodded again.

"I'm not religious or anything, but I said a prayer for your sister."

"Yeah, me too," I said, "I'm not religious either."

He took a hold of my hand, then, and his head wandered back into nowhere land, wishing he was up in Temagami, no doubt, and I stared out the bus window at the farm fields, a hundred thousand shades of burnt umber and dying and dead. In the fall, if you cut away all the trees, there'd be a dead riot of colours, a hundred different shades to dying grass.

The bus shuddered to a halt in the school driveway, and the Woodsman slowly began to pack up. I breathed against the window and tapped my forehead against the fog, waiting for the bus to empty. Outside, I could see Ronnie standing at the edge of the road, talking to a couple of grade nines. Beside me, the Woodsman stood to go.

"Wait," I said.

The Woodsman stopped, turned back.

"Thanks," I said. I didn't ask about his black eye. It wasn't too bad anyway. His latest reunion with his mom and her new boyfriend, I figured, had gone down the same old drain. The difference being that this time, the Woodsman and his brother and sister had their own rooms.

The Woodsman paused, nodded. I guess he'd always been pretty weird about hellos and goodbyes. His sister too. Maybe he didn't believe in them. Maybe he believed that everything always was.

— 19 —

I headed for Ronnie. Traded a smoke with the niner. An Export A for a Benson & Hedges, menthol.

"Nice," I said, inhaling the minty smoke.

"Yeah," the niner said, "there's nothing like menthols in the morning. It's way better than toothpaste." He slipped the Export A I'd given him behind his ear and headed in.

"Do you think he brushes his teeth?" I asked.

Ronnie shrugged. "You going down tomorrow?"

"Yeah," I said, "But I gotta leave at two. It'll take like two hours to get downtown."

"How are you gonna leave at two?"

"Let's skip."

Ronnie nodded. "I don't know if I can go. I've got preggers class. You read the article?"

"Nah," I said.

"Read it," Ronnie said and cocked her head.

She was taking me in as if something bigger than skipping Lamaze was on her mind.

Part Three

— I —

Lora

Two weeks after my sister was gone, the Woodsman put together a memory board. In the details, you could see how much he missed her. He sanded away the rough edges and painted the board a cloudy blue. Before screwing the hinges into place, he stained them with the cold bluing we'd scavenged from my dad's old gun kit, the one that he'd abandoned in a cardboard box in the hall closet.

Ronnie was the first to pin a letter up. But when it rained her words bled from the foolscap and into the grass below. Val had never been one for writing, but on top of the wooden pane, on a stained-blue hinge, she placed a rock. Soon, invisible others had also left tiny stones instead of words. By the time Mel had been gone for three weeks, half a dozen smooth and shiny rocks formed a pile. I never saw who left these stones and came to think of them as the hard pips that existed at the core of the most desperate wishes and prayers.

Val and I met at the board each morning and read any poems and lyrics that had collected up in the night. If anyone thought of scrawling a nasty word on the board, as they had on Mel's locker, the sight of Val, cigarette clenched in her fist, peering through the slits of her eyes at a world gone awry, stopped them short.

I looked at Ronnie's letter, saw the empty space left behind when her words drained into the grass below, and knew my sister was gone.

We all knew. Only no one could tell me what *gone* meant or how long it would last. For a long time, I waited, not knowing what Mel needed most, a prayer against harm's way, an act of sympathetic magic, or an incantation of return. In the end, words were inadequate, the lies we tell to make ourselves feel better, and so, wordlessly, I pinned up the photograph from the Halloween she was twelve, the year that Mel was a kitten and I'd been the one in the big fat peach suit. She'd promised to play James to my peach, but by the time Mom had sewn the last sheet to my bulbous frame, Mel's heart was set on a softly swishing tail. I tore the picture in half, covered her image in saran wrap and tacked it up next to the vacant letter. The other half I tucked in my pocket.

Even with the plastic cover, the colours bled away, leaving only traces. In the blue-green shadows that remained, you could see the parts of the picture that used to be black: the shadow at her hairline, the black dots at the centre of her eyes, the place where her mouth was a little open. Over time, the rest of the image was bleached by the sun and the rain, leaving only traces. Until I saw it, I hadn't known that could happen to a picture. Until I saw it, I hadn't been half so afraid of what could be happening to Mel. If you put the two halves of the picture back together, you wouldn't believe they'd come from the same whole. Except for the way that certain lines still met up.

The Woodsman built the memory board to make us feel better, but seeing what happened to everything we pinned to it made me feel worse.

After the colours bled away, I had the dream for the first time. The dream exists in the same rain-blanched tone as Mel's picture.

In the dream, I'm alone, walking up Roger's Road. It's an old-style road, one of the few hints of the past to have survived all the developments. Roger's Road runs next to the last farmhouse and the last cornfield too. It's among the last haunted places left to us, and so, collects up the neighbourhood's urban legends about farmers and idiot sons, about what is to be found on rusty meathooks in old creaky barns, about the men who crouch among the August-thick stalks, and fondle a passing girl's thigh.

Girls have always dared each other to run through cornfields like this one, and those who stand watch from the edges have always coolly howled, measuring the terrified girl's retreat in a rustling of yellowed heads. Mel and I have done both. We've idled a few steps from the field and let loose unnerving yowls and, as thick leaves slap our faces, in mortal terror, we've smashed through cobwebs and corn plants alike.

Most of the local farms were planted with semi-detacheds before I was born. But there's something of the past at the dip in Roger's Road, where the old tree overhangs, where the acre of cornfield lies. When you stand in the dip, the new houses disappear and you can almost picture the farm as it was a hundred years ago. Two hundred, even.

In the dream, I'm standing by the cornfield and the lane is empty and dark. Ahead of me I can make out what looks like a girl by the side of the road, lying there, her legs in the ditch. The girl's very still.

I can see that the girl ahead of me is gone. *Really* gone. When I look at her lips, there is a hint of blue and her eyes, her eyes aren't any colour at all. They aren't hazel or brown or blue or grey or black. Not now. Not anymore. Her eyes are clouded. Like the marbles we loved as kids. A moment later, the sky clears and so do her eyes. They become as light and blue as the dome above us. I see that her eyes are rounded mirrors and I know that if I look into her road-side eyes, I will let go of my feet, detach from them and simply float away, become first a smudge and then a tiny dot and finally, disappear.

I'm counting backwards from ten when a flutter catches my eye.

It's so small, I don't know that I've seen anything. A second later, the flutter comes again and I see that the girl's blouse is undone and the fabric is drifting open in the breeze.

Only there is no breeze.

It's her chest that's moving, shuddering, as she draws a breath.

The dead girl starts to breathe, and that knocks me up against the real world. I shoot up in my bed, terrified. Bury myself in the Strawberry Shortcake comforter that, the year I turned ten, I truly believed was the one thing I'd want to sleep in for the rest of my life. It may have taken the better part of five years, but nowadays, when I wake up swathed in garish pink, I finally get it: *Sometimes you have to live with what you wish for*.

Still, the comforter makes me feel better. I

dig down into its folds and wait for the shakes to work themselves out of my limbs.

I don't have the dream often, but when I do, I wake up wanting to know more about the girl by the roadside. Her name, even. I have a feeling the girl knows something about Mel.

When I wake from the dream, all I can think about is getting away and if I can, I'll go to the bus station where I can see Mel's image together with the rest of the missing girls. I try to pick out the girl by the roadside, but it's hard, what with how I've only seen her features flooded by dream light, overexposed. I stand and stare at a wall that's been resurfaced with posters, images of a dozen missing girls, and focus on the shape of one girl's eyes, another's lips, hoping for a tremor of recognition.

In the end, what I recognize is this. When it comes to the posters of sweet little kids, towheaded and big-eyed, they're plastered across the five, six, and ten o'clock news. Posters of girls like Mel? So-called runaways? Scotch-taped to the walls of bus stations. I look at the lists next to the pictures, and find that they're written in a dozen different hands, with words misspelled and crossed-out, and these girls, they look almost *pre*-abandoned, as pathetic and sad as those of us who somehow got left behind.

In the girl's can, I sat on the floor across from Ronnie. She dealt me in for a two-handed game of Euchre, and I lost trick after trick. A few minutes before first period, Val came in wearing one of my sister's shirts, her hair uncombed. She nodded towards the handicapped bathroom stall.

The gun was black and heavy and more real than I'd expected. I slipped the thing into my purse.

"You know how it works?" she asked, but I hadn't been watching TV all these years for nothing. It was simple. Aim and pull the trigger.

"Thanks," I said. "Nobody takes me seriously."

"Now they will."

Ronnie looked up when I came out of the stall. I picked up my cards.

"Hearts are trump?"

"Clubs," she said.

Val tapped on a card and I tossed it down. And for a while, I mindlessly threw down the cards Val pointed out, but all I could fit in my head was the weight of black metal. Finally, I handed the cards off to Val and did what I came here to do: stare at the walls and smoke.

I was beginning to think the gun wasn't such a great idea. It was heavy, too heavy, and now that I had it, blanks or no, I knew I'd be too chicken to ever pull it out of my purse. I stood and looked at myself in the mirror. That's the way my head worked. Look at a thing and think, and look at another and think, and pretty soon, I'd forgotten I had a gun at all.

Eyes on the mirror, I reached for the indelible black marker that lives in my lumberjacket pocket, and wrote the words *videri quam esse* across the silvered glass. It was the school motto. Backwards. Like the whole school was. Full of liars and fakes. Outside of these three words, the only Latin I knew was pig. That's when the teacher walked in.

There was so much smoke, it was hard to see her. When I did notice her, I hid the marker. I had the smoke in my hand and, somewhere in my brain, knew that I should drop it, kick it out of sight with the toe of my boot, but I couldn't. Something outside of me, something to do with the paleness of the sun and what it meant to just toss a thing away made it so that the cig stayed put.

Mrs. Pritchard, the Home Ec teacher, swirled into view. The last morning I'd been at school, before Mel disappeared, she'd drilled us on the correct way to place cutlery. A full hour in class, lined up in front of placemats, and all we did was *Set the Cutlery Down* and *Step Away from the Cutlery*. But the only placemats I'd ever seen outside of class were disposable. The kind that line the plastic trays at Mickey Dees, or the ones at the Bonanza Steakhouse with a line drawing of a clown's head, slapped down in front of bawling little kids with a miniature box of crayons.

Val, sitting cross-legged on the floor, looked at me and raised an eyebrow, flicked it. It had taken time, but Mel had learned the same trick. Not me. I'd inherited my eyebrows from the inert end of the Sprague gene pool.

Mrs. Pritchard caught sight of me, and nodded, smiled sympathetically. I nodded back, but signs of sympathy disturbed me. It was the permanence they suggested. I took a drag of my smoke. Reflex, not bravado, and it was only as I exhaled the smoke that I realized what I'd done.

"Melora?"

"Sorry," I said, "Sorry. I'm stressed. Sorry." The cigarette was in my hand still. A tiny column of smoke trailed my fingers.

Val stood and took the smoke from me. I expected her to dramatically toss it in the toilet, some brilliant idea about getting rid of the evidence. Instead, she took a drag herself.

"Yeah," Val said, "I'm pretty stressed too." Looking at Pritchard, Val said, "You're the one with the forks and knives, right?"

Ronnie didn't look up from the tiled floor. She closed her eyes and shook her head.

"We *do* spoons as well, Miss Swynerchuk," Mrs. Pritchard said coolly, "a fact you'd be better acquainted with if you came to class. You know you have to pass my course to graduate?"

Val frowned. I guess she hadn't known.

"Come with me, girls. We'll see what Vice-Principal Haswell has to say."

— 3 —

As she walked us down the stairs, Mrs. Pritchard obsessed over smoking and tender lungs and reviewed the age of majority, and all the while, I was thinking about the cigarette I'd held in my hand, which was just a smoke, after all, a random object, which got me thinking, why not go on and on about the gum wrapper I'd folded in my jacket pocket where it'd been for close to a week now because I'd been wondering, what is it that happens to the things you throw away? Where is it that the things you toss away end up?

I'd always been superstitious, right from when I was a kid. With Mel gone, the feeling had intensified. When I was quiet, I might have looked zoned out, but really, I was thinking. Like the last time I'd seen Mr. D'Sousa, his eyelids had spasmed, the way a horse's flank does when it's bugged by flies, only Mom said they 'flickered' because that would mean he was dreaming, and it was important to her that Mr. D'Sousa be there, inside of his shell, listening. Lately, if I was quiet, it was because it was more important than ever that I work out the difference between a spasm and a flicker, because I was worried that the furniture wasn't made up of dead sticks after all, but that each piece of furniture was a monster in a coma, unstirring, but listening, and because I was scared of the way that things could vanish, like the little stray dog, Laika, we'd learned about in history class, and the flowerpot girl, Katika, and my sister, Mel, all trace of them lost in the dark and empty places between stars.

The night before, Uncle Dave had asked me if something was wrong, and the question, when it reached me, was already a million years distant, the light from a dead star, and besides, what he'd meant to ask was if there was something *more* wrong.

All I could do was point at my head and say, "It's just a little muddy in there."

As I dragged my heels the last fifty feet to the Vice-Principal's office, I focused on the colour of the cigarette pack in Mrs. Pritchard's hand: green. I definitely wouldn't smoke Rothschild's: the black cigarettes with gold tips, which, as far as omens among teenage girls go, is up there with a mixed tape featuring Joy Division and a diary entry that amounts to a suicide note. Definitely Export A and definitely green. I was thinking about Mel when I picked the pack. For a sec, it bothered me that Grandpa had smoked, since he'd died of lung cancer, but it wasn't hard to push him out of my head. In the end, I figured, it's all relative. Since Mel had been gone, it felt like everything was dying anyway.

It wasn't just our files on the desk. Mel's was there too. Hers was a different colour. Darker blue. Vice-Principal Haswell took a long time to speak to us, and let a few minutes pass in silence. It gave a kid a lot of time to think.

Beside me, Val was scratching Mel's name into her math binder with the point of a dead pen. As if writing out my sister's name could call her back or keep her safe or even just shut the pictures out of her head. Val wrote Mel's name, over and over. But if you write something over and over, it becomes strange. Meaning slips away like consciousness after a blow to the head. Val began to scratch the name a third time, and then a fourth, like she needed my sister to exist in this room, somehow, even if it was just on a cruddy binder.

Mr. Haswell closed my file. "Melora," he said, "I know you're having a difficult time. But acting out only hurts you, and sympathetic as I am, it'd be remiss to overlook the longer term changes in your behavior. Two days' suspension, and when you return, sessions with Mr. Muller. He'll help you ... clarify your options."

Haswell said a few words to Val, then, too, and pushed twin envelopes over the surface of his desk.

I picked up my envelope and turned away.

Haswell said my name one more time and I turned back. "I really do hope everything works out with your sister. I'm thinking of her."

Val and I walked out, side by side, and I flooded my head with the guitar riff from "Smoke on the Water." It's all that would come to me. But the music was steady and hard and beautiful, too, in how it obliterated everything else.

– 4 –
Book Report by M.A. Sprague

The boys in <u>Lord of the Flies</u> have the kinds of problems you see in the real world. Before he got shot, JFK goes: "We need men who can dream of things that never were." And maybe that's what the island needed, dreamers, like Simon, people that dream of things that never were. Like John Lennon.

Symbolically, it isn't really an island of boys at all. Everything is a symbol, the island and everything on it and even the watch you are wearing is a symbol. A status symbol, like you said, only status means it'd have to be less cheap. Symbolically, Jack is a guy, like most of the boys, but Ralf handles things more like a girl. Which is why Jack doesn't listen and Simon is definitely a nice girl. I don't know what Piggy did wrong. Maybe sometimes its bad enough to be Piggy.

Sometimes people will look at a person and

go: she's living in her own head. People say that about me. Simon was pretty much that kid too. You got the feeling he was thinking through stuff, that maybe he'd be an artist if he lived. Like a tall and serious girl. The kind of girl that dreams dreams and has ideas of her own about where she'd like to be even if the world is an island and she can't get off of it.

Jack didn't know, he didn't, that you shouldn't hurt other people – it's wrong. If Jack had known that, then the group would have been rescued and Piggy and Simon would still be alive today. At the end, the island would have been more than a lifeless rock. JFK goes "We need people to dream of things that never were." If Jack had dreams, things would have been different. When your dreams die, basically you end up like Jack, broke and messing around, since there's really nothing else to do, anyway.

— 5 —
Lora

The week before Mel disappeared, she'd been under a lot of pressure. She'd failed half of her courses during the school year and had to make them up in the summer and she was late with her last paper in her worst subject, her second helping of grade ten English, and had *three* days in which to make up for a lifetime spent looking at the pictures in comic books and skipping past the word bubbles.

I remember it exactly.

A Friday.

The last day in August.

It was the first day Mel had left the house since being released from hospital the Tuesday before. A few months had passed since Mel and me had gotten tattooed. A week later, Mel would vanish.

That morning, we'd had a fight, a *huge* one.

Two hours later, she'd called me from work to say she was sorry and to *please* bring her my copy of *Lord of the Flies*.

I filled out a job application with fake answers while Mel injected fat, by way of fried chicken, into exhausted housewives and their hip-riding babies. Between customers, I read the important bits from *Lord of the Flies* out loud to Mel.

While I read, Mel and her co-worker juggled chicken parts, thighs and legs, and laughed so loud I had to read the passages more than once. She built her own version of the beast and set the meaty tripod up next to the cash. I remember wishing Mel would stop fooling around, since if she failed general English again, they'd make her drop down to basic. Mel had to be in general if she wanted to go to college for art. Advanced, the stream for kids who went to university, hadn't been presented to her as an option.

It was the second time Mel had studied the book. She loved it, or so she said, but for the life of her, couldn't say anything more than that. Mr. Mewes, the English teacher, gave Mel until the Monday, Labour Day, to find something to say. He'd given her his home address so she could bring it to him right up to nine o'clock the night before.

Mel showed me the piece of paper.

It was weird to know where a teacher lived.

Or that they *had* houses you could visit and say, look through the window and see the teacher inside, no different from a monkey at the zoo. Mel showed me the slip of paper with his address scrawled on it, like a note from some boy, and that made me uncomfortable. I knew if anything happened to his house in the next month, we'd get the blame for it. So far as I know, his house never did burn to the ground.

When Mel's shift at KFC ended, we dragged our feet in the gravelly dust, kicking up clouds all the way to the door of the liquor store. It took maybe a half-hour before Mel found someone she could convince to fetch us a bottle. Mel counted out the money, coin by coin, into his hand.

With the bottle in her knapsack, we headed out for Jules's place.

We were walking up the driveway when Mel started to regret coming. That's when we saw it, out back, next to the shed. Each spring, the pool hall's entry in the Streetsville *Bread and Honey* parade was a sad collection of mange on wheels meant to resemble Snuffleupagus. The float was usually stored behind the local garage for the balance of the year, wheels shored up with cinder blocks, but Jules must've talked the pool hall into storing the old float with him.

We'd been planning to drink in Jules's living room, but this was better.

Inside, it was dim and mouldy. Light fell through screened eyeholes. As we crawled in, the float heaved and lurched, unstable on its wheels. We hunkered down on opposite sides and sat in uneasy balance.

"Fuck, is this perfect," Mel said.

She lit two cigs and passed one to me. Export A. The green pack. "You know," she said, "if we died in here, they wouldn't find us until next spring."

"Mel," I said, "don't, 'kay?"

She pretended to examine her cigarette for flaws, "I'm going to see Dad on Labour Day. Me and Ronnie both. Wilcox is playing the Diamond."

"Monday's a holiday," I said.

"They don't have holidays in jail. The guards don't just take the day off."

"So why are you telling me?"

"Forget it."

With my fingernail, I scraped at the ash on my cigarette.

"It's over with Jules," Mel said.

"Yeah?"

"I've had it with him. *Completely* had it. This morning, I decided to hitch a ride," she said and waved me off, "I know, I'm careful. I'm *always* careful. So, I'm looking back and walking, waiting for the bus or a car, whatever comes first, and this car pulls up alongside me and stops. Everything was moving slowly, and I had this feeling, déjà vu."

"Maybe cause you've, like, done it like a hundred times."

"No, déjà vu."

"Isn't that how you met Jules."

"That's different, that was Jules."

"You shouldn't hitch without a buddy," I said. "Look what happened to Ronnie."

"Yeah." Mel sighed. "Is that really so bad, though? At least she's got the baby now."

I looked at Mel like she was crazy. It occurred to me that they'd let her out of the hospital too soon. "Ronnie's parents are never going to let her keep it," I reminded her.

"Yeah, Mom would never let us keep a baby either."

With a quarter, I began to rub the silver from the foil onto the floor of the float.

"Short version," she said. "Woodrow. All morning, too, I'd been thinking about Jules, I'd been thinking, I have got to change things. I mean, look at the assholes I end up with. Like Jules, right, a total fucking prick. He didn't come to see me once in hospital, not once."

"You got a ride from the Woodsman?"

"I called Jules from the hospital," Mel said, "and *he* was mad at *me*, like it was *my* fault.

Woodrow's different, though. You're always saying that, but this morning, it hit me. Woodrow *is* different. I used to be really happy when we were together."

"You and Kunzli," I repeated.

"I don't mean me and Kunzli exactly."

I helped myself to another of Mel's cigs.

"So you and the Woodsman?"

"Woodrow's different. He's grown up a lot, but still, he's the same in a way. But I don't mean him exactly, just someone *like* him, say. Someone I could talk to."

"Jules isn't so bad, really, if you think about it," I said.

"When Mom drove me home from the hospital," Mel said, "it was surreal. The sky was this dull dead grey. Exactly how I felt. So I'm sitting next to Mom and I'm looking at this dead grey sky and I'm afraid to say a thing, it's like she's made out of glass these days, and I'm sitting there and just, I wanted so badly to just tell her about the sky."

"But the Woodsman, him you can tell about the sky."

"Don't," Mel said, "really. This is important. I don't mean Woody, all I mean is someone different than Jules. Someone smart, book smart even. This school thing, too, maybe I *could* do it."

I shrugged and Mel lit another smoke.

"God," she said, "I'm just tired of this. My life is such bullshit."

"Don't," I said, shaking my head, "please."

Mel looked me square in the face. "I want to be like Trudy Semple."

"Trudy Semple," I repeated, flatly.

"You know, the one who sells flowers for the old folks' home."

"I know who you mean," I said. "Trudy Semple."

I'd always thought Trudy Semple was unnaturally blessed. The kind of girl who gave off the smell of baby powder and linen. Only this month past, after dark, I'd come upon her behind the elementary school we used to attend, sitting by the wall, bloody knees marbled with gravel, eyes shut tight. I touched her shoulder and held out my hand. She let me pull her up. In silence, we walked to the other end of the park, side by side. She went her way and I went mine. Neither of us had said a word.

Next to this mental picture of Trudy, I added one of Mel, with her chronic nightmares of Hiroshima and the A-bomb, acid rain and overpopulation, on the *Streetsville Secondary School Welcoming Committee*.

"Well?" she asked quietly.

I hesitated.

Mel's expression hardened and she looked away, staring at the plywood floor.

"I don't know," I said honestly, "would you *want* to be like Trudy Semple?"

Mel looked sadder than ever and more than anything, I wanted her to be happy. "You could do it if you wanted," I said and even meant it. Mel looked at me, her eyes shining.

"Really?"

"Sure," I said.

I moved towards Mel, but Snuffleupagus dipped and lurched and I had to inch my way back and, with the weight of me, anchor down the opposite side.

– 6 –

When Mel and I slipped out from the trap door in the Snuffleupagus, Jules was leaning against his Volvo, smoking a cigarette and waiting.

As soon as Mel set eyes on him, she looked miserable.

She brushed the dirt from her ass and walked over to Jules, her head cocked to one side, lips drawn in a soft pout. He reached out and pulled her against him and said, "You scared the shit out of me. I thought I was going to lose you. Don't *ever* do that to me again." Jules pulled up her chin when he said it.

Nobody had ever been mad at me that way.

"Hey," I said, walking over.

Jules nodded.

"We should probably go, eh?" I said to Mel. But she was leaning in real close to him and I could tell, already, that it was me who'd go.

"You go on to Ronnie's," she said, "I'm staying here tonight."

"But," I started to say, only I knew it'd be no use. I let my mouth fall shut.

"Cover for me, okay?"

"What about Trudy Semple?" I asked, "What about your English paper?"

Mel shrugged and Jules pulled her in close.

"Can I get a ride, at least?"

Jules tossed his keys in the air and caught them again. Then he opened the back door, and smiled like he'd won a stuffed prize at the fair.

After leaving Mr. Haswell's office, Val and I stopped at the end of the hall on the second floor, next to the girl's can. I gazed out of the window.

"Give it here," Val said.

I handed the letter over and Val ripped the sealed envelope into shreds.

"Now we can both go tomorrow."

I turned away from her, stared out of the window once more.

The sky was the kind of beautiful that steals your breath away. It was the same sky my sister and I had played under as kids. The clouds were soft and fantastical, the kind of shapes dreams take. Whenever I see clouds like that, change-able and shape-shifting and dreamlike, I think of my sister. I was looking out at the sky when Ronnie came and stood next to us. We were all three quiet for a moment.

"Don't you ever go to class?" Val asked.

"They're happier when I skip. I think they feel ripped off, teaching two for one," she said.

"It's funny the way that clouds hang there," I said.

Val looked out the window.

"You got sent down, huh?" This from Ronnie.

"Yeah, but look at the clouds," I said, "don't they look, I don't know."

"Yeah, I should probably get my jacket back, eh?"

"No, Ronnie, I mean, don't you ever look at the sky and wonder about the clouds?"

"Like, is it gonna rain?"

"No, what's holding them up there like that? Like puppets without strings."

Ronnie looked out at the sky. "It kicked me, the fucker," she said, and grinned.

I smiled too and Ronnie placed the flat of my hand against her belly.

"Sure," she said to her belly, "make a liar of me."

"You got a smoke?" I asked.

Ronnie nodded, and after glancing outside one last time, she said to Val, "The jacket."

"It won't rain." Val knotted the sleeves around her waist. "Trust me. I know."

- 8 -

I watched Val's herky-jerk way of ashing her smoke, elbows everywhere at once. People said her mother drank while she was pregnant. Pretty much everyone I knew drank, pregnant or not. Her mom must have drank a lot or drank something weird. Like rubbing alcohol. Or Drano.

I was glad Ronnie had stopped drinking. She was smoking, still, but given the choice, I'd rather give birth to a baby with a smoker's cough than an eight pound alcoholic. Between drags, I pulled at my eyelashes, to see if any were loose. When you find an eyelash on your cheek, you can blow it off your fingertip and make a wish. Loose eyelashes give you wishes, and so does the clasp of your necklace. If the clasp works its way down to the front of your chest, you have to pull it around to the back, while wishing hard. And with each new pack of smokes, if you count out the letters in a boy's name and flip that one over and save it for last, he'll want you. Plus, you can count out the letters when one of your friends flips a smoke down, see if it amounts to their boyfriend's name. Some of the time it does.

"You suspended?" Nancy Tulk wanted to know. She looked at herself in the mirror when she asked, so she wouldn't seem interested.

"Yeah, then Muller when I get back."

"He's for retards," Nancy said, looking me over. She looked interested in the possibility I would turn out to be deficient.

"It's Special Ed," Val said. Val had been in Muller's sessions for two years now. "Special Ed, Nancy. It's not for retards. You don't *have* to be retarded to be in Muller's class."

"Maybe not," she smirked, "but it helps." When Nancy smiled at Val, it was the way Mel used to, and it was like a light struck out all of the darkness in the room. Nobody could hate Mel, no matter what she said to them. Not so long as she smiled.

"Wasn't Mel in Muller's math class?" Nancy Tulk asked.

I looked at Ronnie, who was in Muller's class, but she kept quiet.

"No, she was in general," I said.

"You in gen too?" she asked.

"No, but I'm gonna drop down."

"You coming over?" Nancy asked Ronnie,

butting her smoke on the heel of her boot. She paused to add, "You two wanna come?"

Val shrugged.

"I should probably get home and help out," I said. "Plus I'm meeting the Woodsman."

A silence gathered around his name. Ronnie looked at everyone's feet and Val, she began scratching at her arms again. Nobody looked at me.

"C'mon," Nancy finally said, breaking the silence, "For a couple hours, anyway."

I shrugged.

— 9 —

Val said she'd stop off at the drugstore for breast
pads, since Ronnie was leaky, and the three of
us walked over to Nancy's. In her bedroom,
Ronnie flicked on the stereo, I glanced at the
station call number. The song that was playing
was by Charlie Sexton.

"There's JD. You want?"

"I don't know," I said, worried my mom
would smell it on my breath.

Ronnie shook her head, no, and Nancy
looked at me like I belonged in Muller's class.

"Okay," I said, "I'll have a bit."

I held the glasses, while Nancy slowly
poured bourbon over the sugar cubes.

"Well, what do you think?"

"It tastes like shit," I said. "Sweet shit."

"Don't be an idiot," Nancy said and pointed
to the box. "I mean Ouija." She raised an eyebrow and smiled. She used that same look with
boys, and got whatever she wanted. "We tried it

yesterday and it didn't work, but it takes at least three."

"Three to what?" I asked.

"To use the Ouija board," Nancy said, "I mean, c'mon, everyone's saying it."

Ronnie flicked through the stations on the radio, her face turned away from me.

Nancy unfolded the Ouija and smoothed it flat on the carpet. I stood up and moved away from the board, looking at her bookshelf, tracing my finger across the titles. She had every book from the *Sweet Valley High* series, all with subtitles like *Kidnapped!* and *Deceptions*. Each book in the series had a flag next to the title, announcing what number it was. A good rule of thumb, I've found, is not to buy books with a number on the cover or an exclamation mark in the title. In amongst the pulp, I found one good book. An old copy of *The Secret Garden*. When I opened it, I saw the inititals M.A.S., written in a childish hand. It was like being visited by a ghost.

"Me and Ronnie tried it," Nancy said, "but like I said, we didn't get her. There has to be at least three people," she said, "I mean, you want to know the truth, right? I know I do and I'm not her sister. I mean, don't you want to know if what everyone is saying is true?"

Downstairs, the doorbell rang. I could hear Val talking to Nancy's mom.

"Don't you want to know if it's true?" Nancy repeated.

"If what's true?" I asked.

"The rumours," she said.

I slipped the book into my purse and turned around.

Nancy had placed her two index fingers on the wooden planchette and was pushing it back and forth between *Yes* and *No*. She didn't look up. "People are saying she offed herself," she said, eyes on the board. "People are saying she jumped off the bridge and drowned. Or maybe that she did it in the underwater bunker. Drowned, I mean. That's what they're saying."

Val opened the bedroom door and stepped in.

"My dad says you won't find a body if the person doesn't want it to get found. Like say when a body gets caught down in the water under rocks."

"Jesus fucking Christ," Val broke in, "you're a right piece of work, eh, will you listen to this?"

"It's not me. It's what people are saying. My dad says that when some animals die, you never find their bodies. They crawl off to die. Bears and suicides, he says."

"You dumb fucking cunt," Val said, slowly and quietly, "Could you be a bigger prick? Is that possible. Would it kill you to *think* for a fucking change, to *think* how she *feels* when you say shit like that? Could you think how *I* fucking feel when you say shit like that?

"Don't listen to her," Val said, turning to me. "She doesn't mean a thing. She can't think cause she's a fucking retard. That's all."

"Yeah, I know," I said, "I've got to get home."

Nancy folded her arms across her chest.

"I'm not a fucking retard," she said. "You're the fucking retards. I was only saying what I heard. Don't you even care what happened to her?"

Ronnie put her hand on Nancy's arm and Nancy, thankfully, shut up.

"You okay, kiddo?" Val asked.

"Yeah," I said, "but I might as well head back. You coming?"

Val nodded.

"How about it, Ronnie. You coming with?" Val asked, tossing her the breast pads.

"I can't," Ronnie said, opening the box. "Lamaze."

I looked at her. "How are you going to do Lamaze without Mel."

"Nancy," she said and shrugged. Only Mel was supposed to help Ronnie with Lamaze. It was *Mel's* job. I looked at the floor.

"C'mon," Val said, "Let's get out of here."

"What about tomorrow," I asked Ronnie. "Are you even coming tomorrow?"

"No," Ronnie told me, "It's a bad idea, I think."

Val dragged on my arm, but I pulled away.

"Lora," Ronnie said, "your dad doesn't work for the prison, he's *in* it."

I stared at her, my eyes welling up. It made sense. It made too much sense.

"He's *in* jail," she repeated.

As I turned to leave, I stepped on the up-turned planchette. It collapsed under my weight, useless, but not before one of its peg-legs had pierced my sock, leaving a small pyramid-shaped mark on the sole of my foot. Behind me, I could hear Nancy swearing.

— 10 —

The day after Mel and I had found our way into Snuffleupagus, Ronnie and I hiked out to the railway bridge. Mel and Jules and Darryl had been jumping most of the afternoon. Ronnie was too pregnant to throw herself from bridges and me, I didn't see the point in climbing anything taller than me. Ronnie made a nest of moulted clothes, and I climbed partway up an iron truss, to get a look at how far below the river was, and then clung to the black metal for dear life.

Ronnie lit a cigarette and laughed.

"Jump," she coaxed, "C'mon, don't be a wuss. Jump!"

Bodies were falling all around me. Torsos twisted in the air as they jackknifed, shattering the surface of the river below. When Darryl leapt, he gave a strangled yell. I had to force myself to look down. I'd let go of the truss for a second, but my hands would reattach before I could let myself fall.

Strong survival instinct, I guess.

The three of them had climbed up for another go. All the while, as he was monkeying his way up the trusses, Jules said I'd better climb up, because if I wasn't careful, I'd fall from where I was and what, with the wooden beams below, I'd brain myself. That was enough, I inched my way back down to the platform.

Darryl pointed at a concrete bunker downriver. "C'mon," he said, "Let's check out the salmon trap."

Mel and Jules and Darryl jumped into the river and I watched as it carried them away, towards the grey dot upriver.

Ronnie had taken off her shirt and was applying suntan lotion to her belly and shoulders. The lenses of her sunglasses were pink and each was shaped like a heart.

"I'm going to go with them," I said.

Ronnie shrugged, unconvinced. "Go for it, kid," she said, pulling her sunglasses down a notch on her nose to take me in.

Once I'd made my way under the bridge, I carved a path down to the bank through the blackberry bushes, rocks and thistles. The water was freezing, but in the distance, I could hear the three of them laughing. Their voices made strange, pulled long by the water and made hollow by the bunker's shell.

The salmon bunker was a pale concrete structure, a dozen feet long and rectangular. None of us knew what it was for or how it worked. What we did know was that something in the way the water was drawn through the initial chamber created a powerful whirlpool and a dangerous undertow. There was a hole in the roof over the chamber, and they'd dropped down through the hole into the surging water below. When I got there, Darryl and Jules were holding onto the concrete ledge overhead, and Mel clung to Jules's neck.

I lay flat on the roof and looked down through the hole.

"You coming in?" Jules asked.

"I dunno, is it safe?"

"C'mon," Mel said, laughing and looking up at me. "You've *got* to feel it. It feels like a thousand little fishes sucking on your toes."

I turned around and lowered myself into the hole. All at once, I lost my grip and down I went. At first, it was what you'd imagine it'd be like inside of a washer, during a cold rinse cycle, and I'm a strong swimmer. But soon, it was all I could do to keep to the surface. I tried reaching for the edge of the hole, overhead, but it was impossible to lever myself up and all I got for my trouble was a mouthful of water. I couldn't touch bottom, the roof was out of reach, and I was being sucked under by the powerful current.

I started to panic.

"C'mere," Darryl said, anchoring me to him with one arm.

"Thanks," I whispered.

"Oh my god," Mel said, shivering, "If you drowned in here, nobody would *ever* find you. You'd stay down here forever, swirling round, till the fishes got done with you."

"You're *so* morbid," Darryl said.

"It's true," Mel said, her eyes wide. "It's fucking true."

"Mel don't," I said. "Remember what Mom said. Remember Mrs. Buchanan. You don't want to get put in some foster home."

My sister pursed her lips and shrugged.

Val lit a cigarette and leaned up against the brick wall at the IGA.

"Pull it together," she said. "You can't go home crying."

I wiped at my eyes with my lumberjacket sleeve. I wasn't crying anymore, but my eyes were still wet and swollen.

"I do want to find out what happened to my sister," I told her.

"So what, you want to go back for the occult fest?"

"No, it's just, I tried to talk to Jules. He sort of blew me off."

Val nodded. "You had lunch yet?"

"I could eat," I said.

Val handed me her cig and strolled into the IGA, skateboard in hand. I leaned against the wall, dragging hard on the cigarette, and then ran my fingers through my hair, pulling it forward to hide my face. That's when I saw it, the

Woodsman's old rusted-out Impala, held together with duct tape and string. He popped the door and headed for the convenience store next to the IGA. I slunk behind my bangs, but it was too late, he'd spotted me.

"Hey," he said.

"Not a good time," I said, covering my face with my hands.

"I heard you got suspended. Want me to take you someplace?"

"Yeah," I said, leaning my back against the brick wall to think, "I guess."

Val strolled out of the IGA, a box of sugar donuts in hand.

"You going with him?"

I nodded.

"I'm outta here."

The Woodsman started to say something, but before he could get a word in, Val cut him off, "Don't strain yourself, I live real close."

"Look, kiddo," she said, handing me the sugar donuts, "I'm going to stop at home and see the parents, but I'll be back for dinner." She glanced at the Woodsman and, pointing at his eyes with two of her fingers, said, "Keep your eye on him." With that, she tapped the place where the gun was lodged in my purse, dropped her board and floated down the sidewalk and out of sight.

— 12 —

For half an hour, we sat in the IGA parking lot, eating sugar donuts and watching the rain pour over the windshield, our lips dusted with a fine white powder. The box empty, he started up the car and drove. It was a standard, but the Woodsman held my hand the whole time, snatching it away for a second or two when he needed to shift gears.

When the rain let up, he drove into Memorial Park and shut off the engine. Though the radio was broken, he tapped the heel of his hand against the steering wheel for a few beats, like he was humming a song in his head. The door cracked open and in a single movement he was up from his seat and out of the car. He came around to my side. I guess I would have stayed there, stayed where I was put, but he opened the door and took me by the elbow, pulling me up and out.

The air smelled sweet, like pine trees and

rain. I could see the river from where we were parked. It'd swollen over its banks, flooding the flat basin below.

"I wanna show you something," the Woodsman said and opened the trunk. In it, next to a ratty blanket and sheet, there was a tackle box. He opened it up and pulled out a large gold ring. From it, dangled a dozen flattened plastic O's.

"They're to size penises," he said. "You know, before a circumcision."

The Woodsman put the first of the O's against the tip of my pinkie and then another and another. He stopped when he found one that fit to the knuckle of my finger.

"My dad used to sell them for a living," he said. "Out of the trunk."

I remember the Woodsman telling me that, when he was young and his dad was around still, his mom was an Avon lady and it occurred to me that what he held in his hand, then, was a child-size ring sizer and the Woodsman, the boy I'd been half in love with since grade three, was the schizoid fuck up and liar everybody had always said he was.

The Woodsman closed the kit, but not before he showed me the device used to remove a baby's foreskin. A tubular guillotine. The kind you might use to snip the end off a cigar.

"They just cut it off."

"No anesthetic."

"What a world to come into."

"Fucked."

"No wonder boys are ... you know, assholes," I shrugged. "Are you?"

The Woodsman looked at me. "Am I ... an asshole?"

"No, you know, *are* you, you know?"

"Yeah."

"Did it hurt."

"Must've, eh? My dad said the little things wail."

"That's *so* wrong."

"Wanna see something else?"

"I don't know," I said.

The Woodsman pulled a rig from the tackle box and I watched him slide the needle into his stomach. He needed to, he said, because of all the sugar.

"Wow," I said. "I bet you didn't cry."

"Huh?" he said.

"When you were a baby, I bet you didn't cry. I bet you were tough."

"Yeah," the Woodsman laughed.

In my head, I kept hearing myself say "I'm not in love with you," over and over, a broken record. It made up for the fact that all the Impala had was an eight-track that hadn't worked since 1973, when I was four years old, and the Woodsman's mom used to deliver bags of makeup to ladies in muumuus, as that's what they wore back then, muumuus and bell-bottoms, only I didn't believe what my head had to say.

— 13 —

The Woodsman wasn't at all like other kids I knew. I knew one girl who lied and said she'd had her stomach pumped for alcohol poisoning. But if she had, she'd have known that the hose goes through your nose, and you have to swallow it down, drag it down, into your stomach. And with each swallow, it tears at the inside of your nose. It does not go down easy. It does not go through your mouth.

My sister is the only one I know who's had her stomach pumped. She didn't brag about it either. I was with her the whole time. The nurse told Mel she'd never seen anyone take the hose so easy, but the nurse was a liar. She was lying the way nurses do to fifteen-year-old kids who have eaten a bottle of aspirin, because it did not go down easy. It did not go down her throat.

The nurse put a big silver bowl in Mel's lap, and gave her something that made her sick to her stomach. Only later, did she put the hose partway into Mel's nose. And as soon as she did, Mel gulped and gulped. It was as if she wanted to swallow all of it down, right away. She did it the way a dog treads water the first time it is thrown into a lake. Desperately, out of some innate instinct. Only, if Mel was the dog, it would have looked as if she was *trying* to drown, trying to take the whole of the lake into her so there was nothing left to swallow her up. I held Mel's hand, and I focused on the little S the IV made as it curved, right before it disappeared into her wrist. I think she wanted to pull the hose all the way inside her so it'd stop hurting. That's Mel's instinct. If something's hurting you, bring it so close that it can't or won't want to hurt you. Afterwards, she told me, it was the worst thing she'd felt in her life.

The nurse sucked on the other end of the hose, cautiously, all the time watching the place where the clear hose went into Mel's nose, until the fluid started coming up. And then delicately, as it dripped into the metal bowl, the nurse trawled her fingers through the liquid to make a pill count. Another nurse was on the phone with a bigger hospital, relaying numbers.

I begged them to leave Mom out of it, but they wouldn't listen.

It wasn't until later I got the whole story from Mel.

She'd made a mixed tape with Joy Division, BTO, and The Smiths. The kind of music that would inspire anybody to off themselves. Only she hadn't eaten enough pills and so hadn't died and, worse, they didn't put her away with the punked-out psychos, but kept her on the regular ward in a room directly across from the nurse's station with a window where a wall should have been. So they could watch her, all the time.

Watch, watch, watch.

Not that it did any good.

My mother stood in front the nurse's station, her back to me. She was looking through the glass that separated us, in the corridor, from Mel in the observation room.

I stopped to rebalance the tray at the nurse's station. Something in the way that Mom and Mrs. Nowlan were talking told me to stay back.

"She's not happy at home," I heard Mom say. "Maybe she would be happier somewhere else."

The nurse, Mrs. Nowlan, nodded sympathetically. "I've been doing this kind of work for a lot of years, and I've seen it again and again. Best thing for her."

"Maybe I have been thinking about foster care all wrong. Maybe it isn't such a bad thing.

She's not happy with us at home. That's a fact," Mom said.

Mrs. Nowlan put her hand on Mom's arm, "I'll send the social worker up. She'll help set things straight."

And then Mom's hand covered her mouth, again, and she watched Mel sleep.

"You want to get out of here?" the Woodsman asks.

I look away from the river and nod, and he starts up the car.

When the Woodsman clutches, his engine sounds like the unhappy machine that grinds coffee beans at the Inn.

"Want to head to the dungeon?" he asks. That's what he calls the basement his latest boss stores the lawn mowers in.

"Sure," I say.

The Woodsman heads for the underground.

"Nobody will be there on a rain day," he tells me. "We'll bring the blanket. It'll be like a picnic."

14

We walk past rows of lawn mowers, Weed Eaters, shovels, fat burlap sacks and bags of seed. I pick up a ball of twine. Toy with the rope. I stop by the burlap sacks, six of them, each as big as a teenage girl, and ask, "what's in those?"

"Compost," he says. "My boss gets it from a horse farm in Oakville. The burlap lets the compost breathe. Some people soak it first, in water, make a tea to jump-start the annuals."

"Tea?"

The Woodsman shrugs and holds the door. We slowly climb four flights up to the last un-rented floor in the building. Make our way across acres of eggshell carpet rimmed by smoke-hued glass. In a corner office, he lays down the grungy sheet he keeps in the trunk of his car. There is a small dark stain on one corner.

"Rust," the Woodsman says, following my eyes. "You sure you want to be here?"

I nod.

With Mel's glasses on, everything around me blurs. The details disappear. The way the sheet is white cotton, but not new-white. The age of the fabric. I can no longer see that this office is a cold box furnished only with industrial carpet. I can no longer see how the walls were once painted a milk white. Or that it's the colour milk assumes when it's been warmed and then left to grow cold. I can't see how the paint is uneven because the outlying room is smudged and so, made generous. I can't see the dust that has collected at the edge of the carpet, where it meets the wall. What I see is the Woodsman, who occupies the stark middle ground. I see the Woodsman, and I see the Woodsman's white Fruit-of-the-Looms.

"You're skinnier than I thought," I say.

Around his neck, the Woodsman wears the gold charm that Mel always wore. I look at it and I look at the Woodsman. He looks young, younger than I would've thought, skinnier too. He lays down next to me and I take off the glasses, see the horn that dangles from his neck. The glint of gold.

"That new?" I ask.

"Yeah and no," he says. "Used."

I stare at the charm.

The Woodsman leans over and we kiss. My eyes close and the boy I've known forever, the Woodsman, he disappears too.

15

When he sleeps, the Woodsman is at peace, and has a young face, like a child's. I light one of his cigs, du Maurier, and watch him sleep. The smoke swirls across his skin and disappears.

I tuck one of the Woodsman's smokes behind my ear, and walk out of the office, making my way to the stairwell. Inside, I sit on the steps, look at the gold charm in my hand.

Mel was wrong.

When I get down to the dungeon level, I sit next to a burlap sack and light my last cig. I'd heard about the Keenan girl, whose body had been stuffed into a refrigerator in a rooming house last year. There'd been flowers put up around the door to her house and outside of the place she'd been found. There weren't any flowers around the door to our house.

The stairwell door opens and the Woodsman stands in the open doorway and looks at me. "What are you doing?" he asks. He doesn't sound angry.

"This is Mel's." On my open palm, the gold charm.

The Woodsman touches his neck, his head cocked to one side.

"Where'd you get this?" I ask.

"Pawnshop," he says. He holds his hands out, palms towards me, so I can see they are empty, and slowly, he moves closer. The Woodsman doesn't look angry. He looks afraid for me. As if he's worried that I'll shift my weight to a broken limb and do myself irredeemable damage.

"Do you think I'd have taken something she didn't want to give me?"

The gun is out of my purse and heavy in my hands and still, I'm backing up, edging to the dungeon door. The Woodsman's face is hard in a way I haven't seen before. It reminds me of Val when she's angry, very angry.

"You going to use that?"

I level the gun at him. But all at once, I'm beginning to feel bad inside. Sick. Like I've lost something important but I can't remember what it is I've lost.

"What's in there?" I point at the burlap sacks with the gun.

"Compost," he says. "Horseshit. Fucked if I know. Are you gonna put that fucking thing down, now?" he asks, and takes a step towards me.

16

When I run, there's no thought. Just the rhythm of hitting cement, the shock of it, a jolt carried through spine to the brain, and each time my foot hits the pavement it knocks yet another thought from my head, until pretty soon I'm empty. Running had always felt good, the one thing in this world I was born ready to do.

I kept up a pretty hard pace until I came to Jules's house.

Out front of the shed, Snuffleupagus had been abandoned to the rain. His fur black with mould. I folded next to the furry monolith, hands on knees, and breathed deep. Outside the shed, I saw several bags of Portland cement, flattened, empty, wet with the rain. That's why Jules hadn't been by, he'd been busy putting the cement floor in.

I wanted to ask Jules about Mel's necklace, if the one she wore was a cross or a horn. Only the house was shut up tight and locked with a bicycle chain. They'd left a kitchen window partly open and I dragged a lawn chair over, opened the window and crawled inside.

Nobody was in the kitchen or living room. I walked to the landing at the base of the steps and called out. My voice echoed back from empty rooms. I was alone. Alone and the house was darkly quiet in a way I hadn't ever known it to be.

I backed up, my eyes on the dark stairwell. I let myself out the window and made my way to the bus stop.

— 17 —

Our house was a museum with living set pieces. Mom was at the kitchen table, and Fred Irving was sitting next to her. Uncle Dave was by the back door, looking unhappy to have found himself inside of his own skin. I'd never seen my uncle question his bulk before, but these days, it looked like he was sorry to take up space at all. Out back, Mr. Baxter and Nanna Stokes were oblivious, him smoking cigs and Nanna sipping coffee. She moved at a slow pace. Her gestures softened, dulled, as if she was suspended in aspic.

I came into the kitchen and poured myself a glass of water. Mom came over to where I stood, squeezed my shoulder and gave me a kiss. I gave her a squeeze back, relieved. The school hadn't called her after all.

"How was your day?" she asked, wiping up the ring my glass left.

"Same old," I said.

"You learn anything new?" she wanted to know. I could see time taking its toll. She was leaning on the counter for support. I don't know if she'd slept more than a few hours at a stretch this last week.

"Lots," I said.

"What did you learn?"

"Trig and books and stuff," I said.

Mom nodded and dried the counter with a tea towel.

Mr. Baxter stood in the doorway. He raised an eyebrow and lowered his chin, taking his measure of me. I blinked and focused on the carpet stain, as my brain sorted through the possibilities.

It came up with only one: Mr. Baxter *knew* about the gun.

The school had called. And Mr. Baxter had answered.

Mr. Baxter rubbed his forehead and leaned in the doorway. "Lora," he said, "come out back, I want to see you for a minute."

18

"Did the school call?" I asked.

Mr. Baxter raised an eyebrow and Nanna looked into her hands.

"I screwed up," I said, "sorry."

"She screwed up," Mr. Baxter repeated. "That's the truth. What are you doing smoking?" he asked, cigarette in hand. Mr. Baxter looked at Nanna, shaking his head, "and how do you get suspended before the school day starts? That's a new one on me."

"We haven't told your mother," Nanna said. "She has enough to deal with. The problem is, we don't know what to do with you tomorrow, so I guess we'll *have* to tell her." She looked at Mr. Baxter.

Mr. Baxter nodded.

"Send me to the library," I said. "I could write up a book report."

Nanna and Mr. Baxter looked at each other.

"It's only for one more day," I added.

"Maybe the library's a good place for her," said Nanna. "I could take her to U of T, they have a campus near here. That might not be a bad place for her. For one day."

Mr. Baxter nodded and lit another cigarette. "Oh, and no smoking. Is that clear?"

I nodded and looked at Nanna. "So when were you going to get around to telling me that Dad's *in* jail."

That's when the doorbell rang.

19

When the doorbell rings or the phone jangles off its hook, we stop whatever it is we're doing and wait. It's as if we're surprised to find that the outside world insists it's still there. A hundred tiny heart attacks each day. Eventually, it occurred to me, one of these attacks would be fatal. I walked into the living room and Nanna came and stood next to me. She touched my elbow, and let her hand linger there, as if she was waiting to be led through the house blind.

We could see Claire standing in the hallway now. She was shaking her head and saying something about Mel's chequing account. Mom nodded and their voices dropped. Me and Nanna stood our ground, outside of the circle of hearing, but sometimes, silence was a kind of grace.

A moment later, Uncle Dave called out for me.

"Go on," Nanna said, "We'll talk about your father after you see Claire." Already, her face was regaining its composure.

By that time, I must've made a billion lists. Lists of people, lists of places, and lists of things. But it took Claire to explain to me what they all added up to. I didn't understand everything she had to say, though some of it made sense. I understood the part about grammar. How every absence had a kind of grammar to it. *Rules,* she meant. For how things vanish, the order they vanish in.

"When someone disappears," Claire says, "there's a logic to the questions we ask and the language we ask those questions in."

She was looking through my shoebox as she said this. Holding up one list after another. Some went into the pile on her lap, others she set aside on the bed.

"When someone disappears," she said, "the nouns take on extra freight."

Claire was careful never to use my sister as an example. I guess she wanted to divide the real world from the world of ideas, the way science does. "When there's trauma and identity gets blurred or lost, maybe there's been a massacre of some kind, people come to count on certain of the nouns, personal effects, objects that are strongly associated with the *misper*. I studied the Monongah disaster, back in first year. A mining disaster, at the turn of the turn of the century, in West Virginia. One of the worst. Two explosions trapped hundreds of men and boys in the labyrinth below. The explosions released poisonous gases. Awful, awful thing. And it was the shoes people looked to when it came time to identify the dead. People know their loved ones from a charm carried in a pocket, or a heel of bread. It prefigured some of the work done later, with genocides, with *desaparecidos*." Her eyes drifted off for a moment, and then she continued. "On my first trip to Central America, El Mozote, my first trip abroad as a grad student, I kept hearing this name, over and over, *Desconocido*. I kept hearing it slant, I'd hear it and think *inconsolable*, I'd think *disconsolate*. I heard that name so often, I thought it had to be as common as Jane." Claire shook her head, but didn't explain.

"Mel's things are important," I said, struggling to make sense of what Claire said. It was like she was speaking Greek.

"Absence has its own grammar," she said. "When someone disappears, vanishes, say, and there are no witnesses to the moment, people look to what's left, they organize what's left. If you look to the negative shape, what a person leaves behind, what other absences go along with the central one, you can begin to make inferences. What a person wore when she or he disappeared, for example."

Claire looked at the poster I'd slipped into the shoebox. I'd made a list of Mel's favourite children's stories on the back.

"Mel loved reading," I told her, "until she was eight or ten, then she just hated it. I don't know why."

"It'd be useful if, while she's gone, we could let your sister speak for herself," Claire said carefully.

"I don't understand."

"I said something earlier about taxonomy, remember?"

"No."

"Taxonomy, taxonomy, it means *system*. So, when someone disappears, you organize the *misper*'s environment into types of things, and you take account of those things. Look for related absences. So you know what's gone with him or her. You reconstruct what a *misper* might have taken with them when they disappeared – and just as telling – what they *didn't* take."

Misper was Claire's word for Missing Person. I don't think she knew she used it half the time. The word was haunting, like a song and mist and vespers all at once. It made me wonder, if when you disappeared, something of you, some essential part, might reappear for a little while after the sun rose each morning, only to be burned off of the leaves and flowers as the sun rose high in the sky and its light grew harsher, reached its fingers into the hidden recesses of things. It was soothing too, softer than some of the other words I'd heard them use for Mel. Like 'case.'

"All of those presences and absences," she said, looking at me, "they tell us a story, they construct a narrative. And from that, we can make informed guesses. We can tell whether or not the *misper* was planning to leave the house, and if so, how long he or she was planning to leave for, for a stroll or for a long time, say. And we can trace whether the missing person is active out there now, say, using their bank accounts or sometimes, in official situations, a Social Insurance Number or whatever else might leave little traces in the world."

Claire stopped speaking and looked at me. It was unsettling. It made me replay her last sentence and personalize it somehow. I looked at the floor. "I'm sorry," I said, though she hadn't accused me of anything yet. Mel's birth certificate was in my purse, and I half expected it to fall onto the bed and reveal itself.

"That's what makes it so important that you tell me *everything* you know. You need to tell me the whole truth about everything, not what you think you know about your sister, but all of the details, no matter how unimportant they might seem to you. It helps me make the picture I need. So, no holding back, okay?"

Claire regarded me for a good long minute.

"Good," Claire said decisively. "I think we have an understanding."

I nodded.

"I borrowed her bank book yesterday," I said. "I needed it for something but didn't use it and then today, I borrowed her ID, since you need to be sixteen to visit jail." I said.

"Or donate blood," Val added. I wasn't sure how long she'd been watching, but now, she walked over and plonked herself down on my sister's bed.

"Or donate blood," I said.

Claire didn't look concerned. She waited. Patiently. One eyebrow raised slightly. I knew that admitting to the bank book and ID wasn't enough. She was onto something bigger, though I didn't yet know what.

"My lists aren't like other people's," I said vaguely. "Well most of them are, but not all."

Val squinted at me.

"I make lists of things that don't matter to anyone but me."

"What sort of lists?" Claire asked.

Val wriggled closer to me, and knocked her elbow into my ribs.

"Look, she's okay, I trust her," I told Val and turned to Claire. "I have other lists, lists of *need-*

less details," I said, picking up on a word Claire had used earlier.

Val shook her head.

"Some details can seem unimportant at the time," Claire said, "but later, in retrospect, can be *very* important."

"Stuff Mom can't know," I said, getting to the point.

Claire nodded and Val looked miserable.

"As much as is possible," Claire said, "I'd be willing to refrain from making reference around your mother to details that were ... *needless*. But I have to look, to see which details are unimportant and which might help us learn more about what happened to your sister." I let out a deep breath. I felt better. "You're both young girls," Claire went on, as if considering me from another angle. "I bet you girls both keep journals," she said, acknowledging Val's presence, "and that gets me to wondering, where has Mel's diary gone?"

Val looked at me hard, and I looked back. "It's okay," I told her, "we can trust Claire, Claire works for us. Right?" I asked, looking at her.

Claire nodded.

Val shook her head and pulled Mel's diary from her knapsack and handed it over. I could tell from Val's expression that whatever happened next, it was all on me.

— 20 —

A diary is only one version of an event. The version you make when you're pissed off or in love or otherwise completely blown over by a world you've somehow been born into through no fault of your own. Everyone thinks diaries are the truest version of a person, but that's not the case.

A few weeks before Mel was admitted into the hospital, she began to write less and less in her diary, just like how, when she and Jules had gotten serious, she began referring to things using codes, keeping her thoughts private, at least, the ones she felt she needed to keep private from me. It used to be we were more than sisters, we were twins practically, we were so close. It was like we were one person inhabiting two bodies. Our gestures, the way we cocked our heads when we laughed, the way we each moved through a room, the same. In the Halloween picture from when we were twelve, though she was a slim black cat, and me, a big fat peach almost the size Ronnie is now, we had the same look to us. There were a hundred little tics that we as sisters shared, a language only we knew.

Sometimes, looking on as if I was a stranger, I could see why the police would think my sister had run away. But the truth was, everything *was* different this time – I knew it, Mom knew it – and all anyone else had to do was listen to us and they'd have known it too.

After Claire read the diary, she made a big deal out of it. When Claire showed the diary to Mom and Fred, he made a big deal out of it too. He said that it made the case for him.

"What case?" I wanted to know.

Mom looked at the table, saying nothing. I'd never seen that expression on her before. It was like she was shutting down, shutting me out, not open to what was going on around her.

Fred pushed the article across the table, towards me.

I frowned and picked up the paper. Right off, I could see that he was blaming everything on the Woodsman, because of his background, because of the trouble he'd been in as a kid. Fred was the kind of person that could take little details from a person's life and add them up in a way that was both true and a complete lie. The article said the Woodsman was "a troubled young man," who'd been "kicked out of his parents house when he was eight and had gone through a succession of foster homes." He went on to say that the Woodsman was "haunted by the sudden loss of his father," that he was "*known* to the police," and that he'd "cultivated a drug habit, in himself and, it would seem, the Sprague girl as well." That's what Fred called her, "the Sprague girl." As if he hadn't eaten at our table the day before.

The Woodsman would be home by now, up in his room. Maps of no place drawn on the walls. Intricate, pencil-drawn maps of places that didn't exist outside of his head. I wondered if he'd seen the article yet. I wondered what would happen, too, when his mother saw it.

Even the school had turned on her. Fred Irving had a quote from an anonymous teacher, one who never even taught Mel: "It's a different time, basically, than when we were raised. I see it in the girls, especially. I'm telling you, these girls look at you with zero affect. No emotion. On a profound level, when you look at these girls: nothing. There's a certain ... *nothingness* to them, that's it."

In the article, Fred Irving went on to say that Mel had been "self-destructive," and that, "in all likelihood, it was her deep and abiding unhappiness with her situation that drove her to this troubled young man." Nowhere did Fred say that Mel was normal, that it was normal for teenagers to be unhappy, and it was normal for them to stay out all night once in a while, and it was normal for them to rebel, and normal for them to sulk, and normal for them to try stuff out.

Take my diary, it's as miserable as hers, and *I'm* still here.

Fred told us he would help us and in turn, we'd shown him Mel's medical records and Mom had told him her stories. I glanced ahead and saw he'd brought up the OD too, which didn't exactly give the impression Mel was happy at home with me and Mom.

He'd betrayed us, but there Mom was, holding his hand under the table, and nodding as he spoke of the demands of "journalistic integrity," believing that this article was no more than the sour taste of the medicine, and that the cure was somehow on the way.

After we showed them the diary, it got worse. They took Mel's word for everything, the police and Fred and even Claire, only it was her word when she was in one of her worst moods, and they took that more seriously than anything anyone else had to add, including me.

− 22 −

August 31st, 1984

*I swear to god I'm out of here as soon as I'm sixteen.
There's no way I'm sticking around until they put me
in a fucking foster home. Today all I wanted to do was
go to the library and finish my stupid essay but I could-
n't go to the library because my tube top was gone. And
who the fuck might have taken that you ask?*

Well, let's do tell.

*First she steals the Violent Femmes album I have
to fucking return to my fucking friend and then she
gets a scratch on it. Great. Fucking great. And then my
fucking tube top. I'm so out of here.*

*So she comes in wearing my tube top − and it's not
like she has got any reason to wear a tube top − and
then Mom is like we have to do the fucking dishes before I can go like she wants me to fucking fail English
again.*

*So I say to Lora: It's your job − you do the fucking
dishes.*

And Lora's like: Fuck you – you wash, I dry.

And I'm like: No, fuck you – you do all the dishes, and call it rent, for stealing my fucking tube top.

And Lora's like, you want your tube top, have your tube top and she's standing there half naked and wings the thing at me and yells, I've got dibs on drying, dibs.

So I say, fuck you, Lora, keep the tube top, but you wash and dry and I leave. And now here I am at the stupid library and I can't concentrate on this stupid book which why do we have to read this shit, anyways? What good is reading going to do me when I have a real fucking job outside of K F fucking C. Which is where, essay or no essay, I have to go RIGHT NOW.

I remember that day exactly. I may have borrowed her tube top, but I'd also lent her my jeans the day before, and later that afternoon she called me to meet her at work – to bring her my copies of *Lord of the Flies* and *Coles Notes* – since she'd forgotten hers at the library. There were a couple chairs by the window of the KFC, covered with fake leather, and an ashtray between the leather-covered seats. I sat down to wait for her shift to finish and smoked too many cigarettes, and my stomach felt queasy. I had to fold my head between my knees. In the back, her and Kevin, her co-worker, tossed chicken parts around and laughed.

Scribbled in the margin of Mel's diary, sideways, by the entry for August 31st, 1984, it says:

Go ahead and take off. I'll get it all. Your room, your clothes – all of it. By the way, I listened to your mixed tape and it sucks. Loser.

That's what I wrote when I was mad. It wasn't true.

None of it was true.

So, I'm sitting in the glassed-in box that is KFC. The lights a little bright, sterile. A little kid, five years old, comes towards me. She's fascinated by my spandex pants, because they're shiny like zebra skin. Perhaps she thinks I'm one of those talking animals you find in a book.

I remember what I wore that day, down to the ZZ Top-inspired ankle socks. Zebra-striped spandex, a second skin, bought on a trip to a head shop downtown. Mel's sparkly black tube top, that she'd lent me, and an old pair of black riding boots, knee high, moulded to the calves. Real riding boots. A gift from Mrs. Penchuk on one of those happy, halcyon days when her Valium prescription was renewed. A plaid lumberjacket and over that, a jean jacket with the sleeves cut off.

Behind the counter, Mel's in her polyester uniform, awful burgundy and black, but on her feet, she's got on her shit-kickers. Her hair is dyed black. We did it the night before, from a box, to cover the orange colour she'd dyed it before the hospital.

My hair is usual old mousy brown, and it's frizzled up with the moist air. It's a hot and humid August afternoon, and my bangs, damp from the long walk, have curled up against my head.

The little girl, I remember her too.

She is sweet with big black eyes and features a little too big for her head. Her eyes, so big, when she looks up at you.

And I remember, too, how the little girl stepped over to me, so shy, looking up, and she reached her little hand out to touch my spandex, the zebra skin, like I might be a weird cousin to one of the stuffies that lived on her bed.

Her little hand reached out for me and I smiled. But before she could make contact, her Mom snatched her arm and yanked her so hard that the little girl let out a cry. Her mother is alarmed by me, I can tell. After that, the kid holds onto her mother's leg, looks at me through dimpled hunks of meat with resentment, like I'm an ungrateful animal, one she'd been tempted to feed, but that was revealed to her as dangerous.

At the very back of the diary, folded first in halves, then in quarters, are a couple of white pages, neatly typed up. An essay that would never be handed in or graded. And next to it, another of the Polaroids that Jules took the night we got our tattoos. One I'd never seen. I look at the girl in the photograph. Her face is turning a little away from the camera and she's smiling.

Around her neck, a gold chain. I look closely, try to see the shape of the charm, but the chain is too long and the charm, if it is there, remains hidden in her blouse.

− 23 −
Celia

Karin is thirty-one years old when Fred Irving walks into her house, notebook in hand, and asks, do you trust *this*?

I wonder what he could possibly mean. *This* cradled absence, which is impossible for her to hold? Does she trust *those* around her? Maybe he means to ask, does Karin trust gravity, that it is *this* which is weighing down on her day after day? I find myself wondering, time and again, if he could possibly mean to ask, does *she* trust *him*?

By way of answer, I watch Karin take Fred into her girl's room and show him her girl's things, her room, the curtains Mel picked out when she was twelve. When her girl's been gone for a week, we show him Mel's handwriting, how it formed childish curlicues, and ignored the blue lines assigning latitudes to each blank page.

I watch him hold the diary in his hand, sitting on the bed, as Karin rearranges her girl's abandoned bestiary of stuffed rabbits and bears. The shoes. She shows him those too. Rows of them, neatly lined up, from the smallest of small, crawling toddler shoes she's taken down from the attic to remind herself how they were worn, scuffed on the tops of the toes, from her girl, pulling herself along, not yet able to walk.

At night, unable to sleep, I map out the lampposts that have yet to be plastered with her image. All the while, I wonder about memory. How it is that memory works.

Once it is consigned to memory alone, how do we know something actually *was*? How do we know anything with certainty? I know the Holocaust happened, because buying bread, I see the tattoo on the wrist of the woman behind the counter. I see the tattoo and in that woman's eyes, see the silences that have kept her company all these years. I picture the pages in her family's photo album, depopulated, made blank. I look at the wrist of a woman selling bread and know that that is proof enough.

Every experience must leave some sign.

Karin tells me that when she dreams of her daughter, clock hands run backwards, and *this* is the only warning she has that she'll wake into a world in which her daughter is once more lost.

Fred asks her, does she trust *this*? And he almost imperceptibly inclines his head back. I see him measuring her response. But it is the tilt that is measurable. I could render its truth in the clean lines of mathematics, if I were inclined, make a study of geometry, precisely delineate the shift.

Trust.

I once read, in a magazine, that dogs evolved over the millennia to have larger heads and eyes, endearing them to the humans they depended on for scraps. *This*, I think, *is trust*.

Later, Fred asks me, do you trust *that* boy.

And I ask myself what I know of him.

Trajectory. Distance.

Another mathematical measure. I wonder if it was a simple act of betrayal Fred was after with all of us? Or a premonition? Or the truth?

How can one trust anything or anyone in a world gone wrong?

I remember, sitting at the table and looking Fred over. It was very late and my remaining granddaughter was asleep on the couch.

staying only last

I imagine if Karin does trust, it's Fred's sheer undeniable presence that she trusts.

"*This*," he tells me, indicating his notebook, "is a process. I need each of you to trust this process."

Karin looks up, nods. I look at his notebook and fall silent. Think of Karin's dreams. If she's not up drinking coffee until four o'clock in the morning, it's the dreams that keep her up.

"Dear God," Karin says, "if Melissa comes back, she'll come back changed."

In Karin's dreams, Mel's watch doesn't look outwards, but faces her wrist. The hands run backwards. As if through glass or water, Karin can see the hands sweeping backwards.

In Karin's dreams, time has turned against itself, inwards, and the watch's face has turned away from her daughter's own. In dream after dream, she finds her girl and keeps her close, keeps a close watch for creeping differences of whose genesis she can never be sure. She finds her girl and wonders after her in her quietness, and watches her as she sleeps. Yes, she watches the dreamt girl dream, and yes, she watches her dreamt daughter's eyelids as they twitch and wonders, not knowing, where it is that sleep takes her now.

− 24 −
Karin

Fred said to me, "Pick up the pieces. Move on.
As hard as it was, I did, after losing Marie."
"What pieces?" I asked.
There *are* no pieces.
There's a gaping black hole. At dead centre.
And it's sucking everything in.
There are no *pieces*.

That's how I felt. But there comes a point when
you have to look at yourself and see what's left.
Not what's lost, but what's left. And I need all
that's left. I need my Lora to be okay in this
world. That's what's left.
The other day, I went to the drugstore. Picking up some samplers for my girl. I'm picking
through the bin, and a woman comes up to me.
Our girls had been in Brownies together. Hadn't
seen her in years. Couldn't tell you her name if

my life depended on it. She reaches out and touches my arm. Doesn't say a word. Not one. She touches me and nods her head.

That said it all.

I had no words.

I can't focus in on one moment and say, that's it, that's when I *chose* to accept that Mel is gone. It doesn't work that way. The feeling overtakes you. I *could* feel a change coming. I suspected there would come a time when I *would* know, for certain, she was gone. I thought when that time did come, I wouldn't have a thing left to say. Not to anyone. Not to my remaining girl, Lora. Not to anyone. After losing my first-born, what was there to say? What kind of mother *loses* her girl? I knew if *I* crossed that bridge, I crossed it for all of us. If I let myself be sure Melissa was gone, Lora and me were done for. Whatever was left of us would fly to pieces. What is a mother who has lost her child? There isn't even a word for that.

You lose your parents and that makes you an orphan. You lose your child and where are you then? Outside of language, that's where you are. There's no word for what you are.

Without Mel, I would be nothing.

I remember thinking, if I let myself go there, there's no coming back: Lora and I will be what's left of us. I couldn't imagine being in possession of that knowledge without everything in this world falling apart. I'd imagine myself knowing, and in the next instant, I'd picture myself alone, somewhere far distant, making my way down a thin grey line until this life was done with me.

I don't know that I pictured it so clearly as that. But I did suspect, strongly, that life as we knew it would be over with. Lora's and mine. Something had to give. The impossibility of us adding up any other way was there, there, there, at the back of my mind. To let go of the one was to let go of both girls, of everything I loved in this world, of who I was and what I was. If I let go of Mel, everything I knew, everything I'd come to believe about myself, went with her.

So I didn't *find* grace. This knowledge came at me, as steadily as light crawls across a room. It was heading for me whether I wanted it to or not, steadily, one of many things I could not change. So I waited. I waited for this knowledge to do its business and be done with me. And slowly, the newness of the recognition, the strangeness of the fact, passed over me and was gone too. I am now what I became after that knowledge had truly taken root.

In my mind, I rehearsed the end as I'd seen it coming.

I saw a ghost of myself stand and walk upstairs. Take out an old beaten-up suitcase. I saw myself lay the suitcase on the bed and pack some things, impractical things, a book of poems I'd been given a long time ago, the inscription smudged, unreadable. A book I'd always meant to give to one of my girls, had either shown an interest in such things. A sundress I must have given to the Sally Ann years ago, after my second was born. A dress that had always made me feel water-bright as a girl. It would have looked good on Mel. It had on me, before I was reshaped by my girls, by the sudden on-and-off weight of each. So small and so dense, they were, buried inside of me, like tiny stars. I saw myself pack away a girl's tiny handprint, pressed into a cake of white plaster and a handful of marbles, also water-bright, but small, with brilliant fiery cores. It wasn't peace that came to me, then, it was the advent of a cold fact. One that cooled and stilled something at my core. I knew my girl was gone. Irretrievably. I knew that there was not a thing in this world to be done about it. That fact came to reside, here, in me, at dead centre.

In my mind's eye, I took out my very best things, and hers, and packed them away in an old suitcase. Somehow, that helped. Putting these bright things away from me helped. Such tiny sacrifices. And with each tiny thing that went into the suitcase, I said goodbye. I held each glass marble in my hand. Gave up the fiercely burning star at its centre. Saw it buried in the lavender silk folds that line the sides of old suitcases, and as I let go of the best, most prized things to a child, I let go of the child. She let go of me, too. I could feel it. I knew then that I would go on and that I'd go on in spite of yet another indifferent fact, that the truth is, there isn't a place in this world to go from here.

— 25 —
Lora

Uncle Dave saw Claire to the door. "I'm sorry, but I'm wasting time here, yours, mine. I won't take anything for what little I've done. I'm sorry," Claire let the thought trail off, and shook her head.

Uncle Dave tried to bridge the gap that was daily growing between me and Mom and the world that went on without Mel in it. He came almost every weekend, to have dinner with us, and most of the time, he brought his girlfriend, Jenny, too. Jenny I'd always liked. She was a hairdresser and would cut my hair in any style I could pick out of *Seventeen*. I was glad to have Jenny, more and more, since Mom found it easier to talk to her than to most people, and because nights, if Jenny and Uncle Dave weren't here, Mom waited to be left alone so she could smoke cigarettes and drink in the dark, as if, with no one there to see, she wasn't drinking at all.

At night, until we were twelve or so, Mel and I used to crawl into Mom's bed, the TV on. And she'd comb her fingers through Mel's hair or mine, parting and reparting it, as we watched *The Love Boat* or *Fantasy Island* or whatever else was on, even the ten o'clock news. After Mel was gone, Mom and Uncle Dave bought me a small television set that I kept in my room and Jenny would come up after dinner, and the two of us would watch whatever there was to watch while Dave tried to sort out Mom downstairs. I remember these times as some of the few moments in which I felt almost peaceful, like everything had been emptied out of me and with the TV on, there was nothing left to be said.

With her boots and glasses recovered, I both knew and didn't know the worst, but here, in the quiet dark, with a flicker of images reflecting off my pupils, my view of the world shrank to the size of this one small room.

The continental divide in my life, the one that marks the great split in life, was the night Claire gave up on my sister, the night Claire gave up on me.

I remember, I smoked a cigarette right before and after she left us, to mark the dividing line in my life with more than the queasiness I felt. On one side of the divide lay the past, on the other, my future, if I decided to have one. I stood there and smoked and measured time, finding it incredible that only a few hours had passed since the Ouija's planchette had bitten my heel.

Looking into my future, as far as the eye could see, was life without Mel. I pictured it as a slowly greying desert, punctuated by sessions with the remedial teacher, Mr. Muller. I didn't yet know that Mr. Muller would remind me of my love of writing, and so, would save me from myself. According to my vision of the future, the one I feared was being carved out for me at school, if I was lucky, I'd graduate from basic courses with some of the skills required to flip a burger. And at best, well, I didn't know what 'at best' might look like, except through the inconstant images I saw on TV.

Uncle Dave saw Claire to the door and out of our lives and Jenny, she put dinner on and Nanna Stokes, she peeled the skin from mute vegetables. Mom helped lay out the dinner table, but as the food was being set down, she held up her finger, as if she'd only be gone only for a second, long enough to get napkins or a tea towel or something to put under the potatoes. And then she was gone, the way she is sometimes now. Her dinner congealing into a mass, with a warm heart at its centre, and Mom, shrugging it all off to go upstairs, casually, like there was no need to mention going, since she'd be back in a moment. But she wasn't back in a moment. She's never back in a moment. And at first, you think, she needs to get something out of the closet, and then you imagine that she's in the bathroom, only such a long time passes and she never comes back.

After scraping the lump that was Mom's dinner into the trash, Uncle Dave asked me to say goodnight for them. I went upstairs and found Mom lying on my bed, the TV off, which was a rare and strange thing. I came in and sat on the bed beside her. And it was so quiet, what with the television off, that I knew.

"There isn't a God, is there?" I asked.

Mom looked at me, carefully, and I could tell it was Karin doing the looking, and that Karin Sprague was a person apart from my mom. That Karin, though a grown-up, had once been a teenager like me, and maybe she'd been around a lot longer, but this Karin was bewildered by a world that was basically fucked up beyond comprehension. It was not a mom talking to me now, at least, not a mom who pretended things could be made to make sense with enough effort.

"No, honey," she said, "there's not."

We were both quiet.

"I could braid your hair," I said, and Mom nodded and I went to get the brush.

I propped up a pillow behind me, Mom rested her head in my lap and I pulled her long wavy hair from the tight elastic and began to brush it out. There were no tears, and she made no sound, but I had the feeling that Mom was crying as I counted out the strokes to a hundred, the way Jenny had taught me. Already, I knew I'd keep going long past a hundred, for as long as she would let me. As I brushed her hair, I saw that Mom wore Mel's charm around her neck and that Mel's charm took the shape of a cross.

Mom rested her head on my lap and I brushed out her hair, right there, in the absence of any God to bless us or curse us, and in the dark mirror the television made, I saw us dimly reflected back, and it was her and me, and what was left of our lives.

Acknowledgements.

I am grateful to Mike O'Connor, for having provided the home this work could come to, and for always trusting the writing first. Thanks also belong to Jon Paul Fiorentino, the editor of this book, for his incisive eye and for so strongly believing in the writing. I'd also like to thank Gillian Rodgerson for her meticulous copy-edit.

Books are written over years and exist in the context of conversations, some sustained, and some occasional. For conversations of the sustained kind, I'd like to thank Wayde Compton for being there, always, and for being this novel's first, last, and best reader, and Rob Allen, whom I very much miss, and who was always among my best readers, and always, my good friend. Thanks also to Jean Baird, Julie Boulanger, Margot Butler, George Bowering, David Chariandy, Amber Dean, Roger Farr, Reg Johanson, David Hoe (for the etymology of science and shit), Joseph Holland (for, as a child, having warmed the wings of a bird), Ryan Knighton, Francesca

LoDico (for her n^{th} hour eye), Glen Lowry, Amanda Marchand, Lora McElhinney, rob mclennan, Aaron Peck, Christopher Petrov (for his tour of Streetsville Secondary), Renee Rodin (for parsing the title with a poet's eye), George Stanley (because I've always wanted to be that tall and serious a girl), Michael Turner (who introduced me to the work of Nancy Burson) and Karina Vernon. I'm also grateful for the support of my families.

Among the many sources I read, I am especially indebted to Robert DeYoung's doctoral dissertation, "Ultimate Coping Strategies: The Differences Among Parents of Murdered or Abducted, Long-Term Missing Children." His text includes the narratives of parents who've lost their children, fragments of which filter into and inform Karin's chapters (Joan, whose eleven-year-old son was abducted, says: "At some point you get to looking at, not just what's missing, but what's left. And I was desperately wanting to hold on to some of what's left"; and Lynn, whose four-year-old daughter was murdered, says: "There are no pieces to pick up. You just had a great big hole torn into your life — there are no pieces. There's a great big, gaping vortex that's sucking everything in.")

Early incarnations of this novel, unrecognizable as such, have appeared in *Fourteen Hills*, *Sling Shot magazine*, *The Capilano Review*,

Side/lines: A New Canadian Poetics, *You and Your Bright Ideas* and on *Brave New Waves*. Recognizable ones have appeared in *Twenty-five years of Tree*, *West Coast Line* and, again, *The Capilano Review*.

Most character names are recombinations of first and last names, drawn at random, from my high-school yearbook, although none of the characters in this book are based on real people.

I would like to gratefully acknowledge the generous support of the Canada Council for the Arts and the British Columbia Arts Council. Thank you for giving me the time to write this book.